Dear Reader

a novel written by

Lukwanna Littlejohn

Library of Congress Control Number: 2005904624

Copyright © 2005 by Lukwanna Littlejohn

All rights reserved. No part of this book may be reproduced in any manner whatsoever without written permission, except in the case of brief quotations embodied in critical articles and reviews.

Cover design by Darlene Schacht, Art Bookbindery.
Author's photograph on back cover by Laurie Friedman

Printed and bound in the United States of America by A&A Printing
www.printshopcentral.com

Published by Black Pen Press

ISBN0-9769863-2-9

To My Family:
Daddy, Mother, Krieta, Jaelyn And Nicole

Acknowledgements

First and foremost, I'd like to thank The Almighty for giving me the pen and my parents for giving me the crayon; Cole, for introducing me to the ocean; Mother, for teaching me the power of the written and spoken word; Daddy, for passing on the coveted gene of writing; Krieta, for believing in my vision; and Jaelyn, for showing me that miracles do happen.

I'd also like to thank all those who were with me during my writing process: Mr. Kennedy, for helping me tame my voice; Dr. Trissauna Larson, for listening to my dream before it became reality; Zami, for showing me ATL love; Art book bindery, for your professionalism and spirit; Kristin Gassner, for your dynamite logo design; and Nicole Denison, my copy editor, for helping with my struggle against dialect versus grammar.

And last but not least, I'd like to thank the readers and writers of the world: Audre Lorde, Alice Walker, April Sinclair, Toni Morrison, Zora Neale Hurston, Terri McMillan, Virginia Woolf, Langston Hughes, James Earl Hardy, E. Lynn Harris, Walt Whitman and all the other writers who made the impossible happen.

And to those who I did not mention: You're still in my heart even though my page is full.

May Connie and Kendall live in a society free of hate.

"A Persian cat is not enough. I must have a motor car."
Virginia Woolf, *Professions for Women*

Prologue

"How do you feel around him?"

"What do you mean?"

"I mean, when he comes home from work, what goes on in your head?"

"I don't know."

"I think you do, Kendall."

"Well, I don't."

"Does he make you mad?"

"Sometimes."

"What does he do that makes you mad?"

"I don't know. I guess it's just his whole vibe."

"His vibe? Elaborate on that."

"Well, he comes home from work, grabs a beer and heads straight to his room. He doesn't even want to talk to me at first."

"At first? So he talks to you later?"

"Yeah. It's almost like he won't talk to me until after he's had his beer." I paused to scratch my eyebrow. "I take that back. He does say, 'Hi. How was your day?' Then it's off to his room."

"And how does this make you feel inside?"

"I told you already. It makes me mad."

"Okay. So what happens after he's had his beer?"

"He comes out to see what's for dinner."

"Then?"

"Then he comes in the living room to talk."

"About what, usually?"

"Usually, just about shi-" I covered my mouth in embarrassment. "Sorry. It's becoming a habit."

"What is?"

"Cussing. It's funny, too. I used to be able to control what I say but lately it seems like the words keep taking over my mouth. Sorry."

"Don't apologize, Kendall. Sometimes we use profanity to show how we feel. It's obvious you're angry. By any means, say what's on your mind. Profanity doesn't bother me."

I smiled. I guess Dr. Porsche wasn't that bad. I mean, she had already been my therapist for six months. I really didn't know if the ninety-dollar-an-hour sessions were working. But I was ready to try just about anything. Know what I mean?

"Kendall?"

"Yeah?"

"Back to what you were saying about your father. What do you talk about when he gets home?"

"Nothing really. Just your average shoot-the-breeze kind of conversations."

"Do you enjoy these conversations? Even if they're just to shoot-the-breeze."

"A few years ago, we barely talked at all. So I guess I do enjoy the little time we do have together." I partially covered my mouth with my left hand. "Despite the fact that he's always buzzed by the time we do talk."

"What did you say?"

"I said, I enjoy the time we-"

"No, the last part."

"Oh, that. He's usually already full of alcohol by the time we do get to talk."

"And how does that make you feel?"

"I told you. It pisses me off." I clutched the arms of the blue, velvet couch.

"Let's go with that anger, Kendall. Why does it piss you off?"

"Because."

"Come on, Kendall. I know this is a touchy subject but it'll really help us move on if we can get to the bottom of your anger."

"I don't know why it pisses me off. I don't know why I get irritated whenever he comes around. I don't know why he can't be around people unless he drinks. I don't know why it seems weird to see him drink water, or soda or juice. I don't know why he always reeks of beer or brandy. He drinks it straight out of the bottle ." I exhaled and released my grip from the couch. "I just don't know."

"It definitely sounds like you know."

I smiled.

"One more question before you go."

"What?"

"Have you ever asked him to quit drinking?"

"Asked him? Of course. But he has to want to quit himself."

"Does he know he has a problem?"

"I think he knows. But maybe he feels like since he's not hurting anybody physically, it's okay. Know what I mean?"

"Yes, I do. But unfortunately it's the mental aspect that's doing the most damage."

I stood up and grabbed my purse.

"See you next week, Kendall. Continue to write in your journal at least once a day. Write whenever you feel too frustrated to talk."

"In other words, I need to write every damn minute, huh?"

"If that's what it takes, Kiddo."

chapter one

Unfashionably Late

I should've known he'd be late, again. I should've known the moment he said, "be ready at seven o'clock," he actually meant eight or nine. For the entire year Darius and I have shared as one and a half beings, he's never been on time. But I guess that's typical for the male species. I mean, in the nineteen years I've been on this sphere of madness I haven't once met a man I could rely on. So, for the umpteenth time, I was all jazzed up with nowhere to go. Damn, Darius. You'd think he'd at least have the decency to call. After all, he was an hour late. I didn't have time to be sitting around waiting for his late behind. Especially not in my parents' house, also known as my house, with Mother giving me the hundred-question pop quiz.

"Where's he at, Kendy? Where you goin'? What time's he supposed to be here?"

As if I wasn't already mad and irritated enough, good old Mother was there to push me over the edge a little more. Instead of responding to her questions, I nodded my head and smiled every few minutes to make it look like I was interested in what she was saying.

And like every other male-identified irritation in my life, I can't help but subconsciously blame one man: Thomas J. Reed, a.k.a, Mr. Unreliable. But I can't be too mad at the guy; he does share partial responsibility for my existence.

My father was the first person I laid eyes on when I was born. Apparently, the instant I exited the beautiful warmth I now identify as Mother, he was there to greet me. All seven pounds and eleven ounces. He was responsible for separating the one tie that physically bound Mother and I together. In other words, with sweaty and shaky hands he bravely snipped the umbilical cord. At the same time, he pulled the three of us closer together. It was a beautiful experience. Or so I was told.

I've known Thomas and Carla Reed for nineteen years and counting. I'm proud to have known them for so long because parents can teach you a lot. I learn new things from Mother almost everyday whether I want to or not. She taught me how to be a woman: A beautiful, strong black woman. Even though some people say I'm a tomboy.

I'd have to blame the tomboy part on Daddy. He's the one who taught me to catch a softball and cast a fishing line into the water. Mother hated it, too; she didn't want Daddy turning her "baby" girl into a boy so she intercepted his innocent intentions by buying me dolls and soft girlie crap. But when given the option, I preferred robots to dolls. I guess being a tomboy runs in my veins. What can I do?

My sister, Kiara, was introduced to the world six years before I was. She was my parents' first child so Daddy didn't give a damn whether she turned out to be male or female as long as she was healthy. But after I was born, Mother found out that I was going to be her last child; the doctor told her that due to cystic ovaries she was going to need a hysterectomy. I later learned that Daddy wanted a boy. Too bad. He got me.

I think Mother has always been worried that I would "turn out" gay. In the fourth grade I hung around nothing but boys. I wore baggy, bright-colored shorts that went passed my knees and T-shirts with corny phrases like, "Skate a Pool," or "Skate or Die." And let's not forget about my Bruce Lee skateboard that I rode around on in place of my pink bicycle that Mother had the nerve to buy. I still have the scars on my legs to prove it.

I don't think I've ever been mentally attracted to a guy. But I have to admit, some men are pleasing to the eye. I think that may be my problem. What kind of relationship can you base on physical attraction alone? Know what I mean? It seems like I always meet the perfect man, physically, then he opens his mouth and starts shooting out ignorant phrases that irritate the hell out me. I've been forced to end many relationships for that reason. I'm not saying that I'm sleazy and like to sleep around. I'm also not trying to be conceited, either. My skinny, butterscotch-colored frame is an acquired taste. Most men, especially Black men, like a woman with a little meat on her bones. And let me tell you, besides a second of rump and a minute of hips, my body resembles a bean stalk. But some guys find my lean body sexy. Like I said earlier, it's an acquired taste.

Even though I've "talked to," or for you squares out there, "dated" a fair number of guys in my day, few really hold a special place in my heart. I can count the number of guys I've gotten serious with on one hand. There was my first boyfriend, Nate. He looked just like a teddy bear. I could've probably fallen in love with Nate if it wasn't for the fact that we were so young. I mean, what do fourteen-year-olds know about love? Probably the same thing most adults claim to know about love.

Next on the list was Kenny. I was sixteen and never loved him. But I did love the way he wore his jeans hanging off his dark behind. Although I never saw his behind to even know what color it was. The reason why Kenny and I never made it is because he didn't have any goals. I know most sixteen-year-olds don't have a clue as to what they want out of life. But, hell, he didn't want to do nothing but lift weights and call me on the phone every damn minute. Which led me to another elimination factor; I needed air. Let me up for a minute to breathe. Know what I mean?

Tony came next. He was tall, rusty-brown and had the prettiest smile. I think maybe if I would've been with Tony for more than two months, things might've worked out. Unfortunately, he dropped out of high school his senior year and I never saw him again. It's a classic American love story. Don't you think?

My last relationship link is Darius Mayfield which finally brings me to the present. Darius and I have been together for one year in counting. According to him, we met on January ninth of 2000, exactly one year ago today. I believe it was at a party, no, it was at Chocolate City, the only hip-hop club in Dryton. I was standing at the bar, ordering iced coffee, when he bumped into me, causing me to spill my drink. I know this sounds like your typical movie-type meeting, but I'm telling it exactly the way I remember it. He was wearing a black button-up shirt with khakis and I was wearing my drink. The only striking feature I noticed about him, since it was dark, was his voice. Let's just say, if I would've closed my eyes, I'd have sworn I was meeting Barry White. If it wasn't for Darius' voice, we probably wouldn't be together, today.

    I just hoped, tonight, his reliably-late ass made it to my house before I fell asleep. I had a long day. The first day of a new semester is always exhausting. Not to mention the fact that my best friend, Tomeeka, made me late for my first class. Check this out: at seven o'clock this morning, she called and asked me for a ride to school. But when I got to her apartment, she took an extra half-hour making sure her appearance was up to the Dryton State University social code. I mean, shouldn't she care more about her grades being up to code? That's the problem with young folks today. Not enough realize the importance of higher education. Know what I mean?

*   *   *

    When eight o'clock rolled by, I started thinking that maybe Darius wasn't going to show up. I've never been the type of person to sit around and wait. It's not my style. Besides, I was looking especially swanky at that moment, if I don't say so myself. Instead of my usual, casual attire, I was dressed like a traditional lady. I'm not saying I'm usually not a lady. I just feel more comfortable in jeans and boots than I do in skirts and stilettos. Anyways, I had on black slacks with a white blouse that draped across my B-cup breasts perfectly. I have to admit, I was looking good. And my skin was lightly coated with perfume so I smelled good. But it was already eight-fifteen and Darius still wasn't at my door. I started to worry. What if he was involved in a terrible wreck? Or what if some crazy lunatic held him at gunpoint, stole his clothes and left him butt-naked on the freeway. I shook my head. Darius wasn't in any trouble except for the trouble I was going to give him when he showed up, if he showed up.

    "That boy still ain't here?" Mother waltzed nosily into the living room where I was sitting. She had on a red, terry cloth robe with nothing else underneath. As far back as I can remember,

Unfashionably Late

Mother's hated clothes. If given the chance she'd go to work naked everyday. But I guess it would be bad for business if the owner of the first African-American bookstore in Dryton showed up on the premises in her birthday suit. Don't you think?

"He's late as usual." I smoothed down my jet-black hair and inhaled deeply.

"I swear that boy will be late to his own funeral."

"Ain't that the truth."

"You work tomorrow?"

"Eight to four."

I hate wasting my weekends behind the lens of a microscope. I mean, I'd rather meet, Muffin, the cat dying of renal failure. Instead, I get to count Muffin's elevated white blood cells or send her tissue sample to the pathologist for evaluation. I mean, is Muffin a lovable or a fractious cat? Will Muffin's owners do all they can to save her or will she soon become the lifeless victim of euthanasia? But I guess you don't earn the title Veterinary Laboratory Technician 1A for patient interaction. Know what I mean?

"I don't want you out late, tonight. You know what happens when you drive to work tired." She tightened the belt on her robe. "I can't take another call saying you got in an accident. Once was enough. My heart can't take much more."

"Mother, it ain't gonna happen, again. You know I didn't get but two hours of sleep that morning. Dang."

A year ago, I fell asleep at the wheel while driving to work. Nobody was hurt except for the raggedy fence I hit on the side of the road. Still, Mother won't let me live it down.

"Just humor me and try to get home at a decent hour."

I sighed in defeat. "Okay, Mother." I looked down at my watch. Damn. It was already eight-thirty. It was obvious Darius wasn't coming. I stood up from the couch and walked back to my bedroom to grab my coat.

"I'm gonna go meet the girls at the club. Ain't no use waiting around here."

"But you know he's gonna be here, Kendy. At least call him."

"He never answers his cell phone. And you know I ain't calling his house. His step mom has horns."

"She get bad with you?"

"No," I answered with a shrug of my shoulders. "She just acts like she has a stick up her ass-"

"Kendy, you know I don't like when you talk like that."

"Sorry, Mother. But she don't even like Darius."

"That's a shame. Where's his real mom at?"

"On the street somewhere trying to get a hit, no doubt."

"She's on crack?"

"Yeah," I said, sliding my jacket around my shoulders.

"That's too bad. Darius turned out okay, at least."

"Then where *is* he?" I leaned over and kissed her smooth cheek. Mother's skin always has reminded me of hot chocolate: Rich and creamy.

"Well. I guess you have to do what you have to do. Be careful, though."

"I will. What time does Daddy get off?"

"Eight-thirty. He should be home any minute-"

"Who should?" A familiar voice cut in.

Just as I was about to walk out the door, Daddy walked in. He had on a cream-colored shirt and a dark-green tie. I've always loved the way Daddy looks in green. It brings out the color in his hazel eyes.

"Hey Daddy." I leaned over and kissed his almond-colored cheek. A small amount of stubble scratched my lips.

"Hey, Kendy. What you all dressed up for?" He leaned over and kissed Mother on the lips.

"I *was* going out with Darius. But it looks like my plans have changed."

The familiar sound of the "pop" of a beer can drowned out my answer.

I rolled my eyes. First Darius, then Daddy. Would I ever be able to trust men?

* * *

"He jus' didn't show up?"

I sat in the crowded club with my two best friends, Tomeeka and Keisha. Chocolate City is the most happening club in

Unfashionably Late

Dryton. Actually, it's the only hip-hop club in Dryton. So every hip-hop fan from the California Valley was in the house.

"Yeah." I looked Tomeeka directly in her light-brown eyes and took a sip of my cola. "Just didn't show up."

"There has to be an explanation though, Kendy. That don't even sound like somethin' Darius would do." Keisha raised her right, overly-plucked eyebrow in disbelief.

"Well, he did it. And at this point, I don't even give a damn. I'd rather be single than deal with this mess."

"No you don't." Keisha laughed loudly over the bass-booming funk that shook off the walls.

Tomeeka and I joined in the laughter.

"So what you gonna do?"

"I don't know, Meeka. I'll see what he has to say. But I might end up letting his behind go."

"That's one fine behind to let go."

"Then you be with him, Keisha." I rolled my eyes at her.

"I don't want Darius. I jus' said he was fine. I got plenty of men. I don't wanna settle for jus' one."

"What men, Keisha? Don't forget, I live with you. Ain't nobody been callin' your big ass lately."

"Screw you, Tomeeka. Plenty of men love this thick body." Keisha stood up and started grinding her big butt to the music.

"If thick, by definition, means big as a house."

Keisha flipped Tomeeka off. Her middle finger resembled a jumbo-sized Tootsie Roll.

"Relax, ladies. Damn. Can't you two be together for a minute without getting ethnic'?"

Keisha sat down.

"Shut up, Kendy. You know you be gettin' ethnic, too," Tomeeka said.

For those who don't know, getting "ethnic" refers to the rambunctious attitudes that white America seems to think most African-Amerikan's display. And quite honestly, I'd have to agree. We don't like to take things laying down.

"Tomeeka, I know you didn't just try to school me. I was the one who was late to chemistry because of your slow behind taking an hour just to get dressed."

"I said I was sorry. It ain't like I did it on purpose."

"I know. I just wanted to let you know."

"For the hundredth time."

"What? Don't make me have to raise up on you." I took another sip of cola. "What happened to your car, anyway?"

"It's a long story that ends with a certain brothah named Marcus."

Keisha and I both shook our heads in unison.

"Say no more, Girl." I tried to sound sympathetic but the story was getting to be old. Marcus is Tomeeka's roughneck boyfriend. They've only been together for a year and he's already broken her arm, busted her jaw and stolen her car twice. To say they have a love/hate relationship would be an understatement. But that's the life you have to prepare for when your boyfriend is a drug-dealer. You either have to deal with it or get the hell out. Know what I mean?

"I'll take you tomorrow, Meeka. I got an early class. Even if you *are* jealous of me."

"Jealous? Of what? All that fat rollin' off the sides of those tight jeans? Damn, Girl, you could've at least found a shirt to fit over that belly. Lookin' like a dairy cow."

Keisha stood up, sending her chair flying back a few feet. "Trick, that wasn't even called for. Didn't nobody say nothin' about that nappy horse hair you got thrown on the top of your head."

Tomeeka stood up and got in Keisha's face. "You see a trick, you knock her down."

"Come on, now." I stood between the feuding buddies. "This is ridiculous. You guys don't wanna get kicked out, do you?"

"I wasn't mad, no way. She's the one who got funky for real." Tomeeka sat back down. "With her big self."

"Don't hate me 'cause I'm beautiful."

I watched silently as they continued to argue back and forth. I looked around the musty room wondering why I was even there. I've always been more into Prince's greatest hits than hip-hop. Don't get me wrong, I dig hip-hop just as much as the next girl. But you're more likely to see me rolling down the street in my drop-top convertible bumping "Purple Rain" over any rap song.

"You wanna dance?"

I recognized his deep, baritone voice right away. Like smooth, liquid jazz.

"Darius? What the hell are you doing here?" My eyes were rolled and my hands were folded tightly across my chest.

"I came to see the woman I love but I hope she's not already gone. I wouldn't want her to leave me."

"She should leave you after the way you treated her." I rolled my eyes even harder. Although, I have to admit, he did look cute with his golden-colored skin and dark brown locks.

Keisha and Tomeeka leaned in closer to get in the business.

"That's true. But not after I tell her what happened. She's an understanding woman." He parted his lips into an apologetic grin. His teeth were gleaming white with a crooked front tooth that added character to his physique.

"You should've called, Darius. I waited an hour. I even dressed up for you."

"You look beautiful."

"That was cold-blooded. It's our anniversary."

"I know. I'm sorry, Baby Girl. I found my mom under the bridge, again. I tripped. I hate seein' that shit. You know?"

The bridge is a place in downtown Dryton where crack fiends hang out waiting for their next hit. It resembles one of those dirty slums you see in movies that always smells like piss.

"How'd you know I was here?"

"I know my girl," he said, grinning from ear-to-ear. "Besides, your mom told me."

I laughed. I couldn't be mad forever. At least he had the decency to find me. Know what I mean?

"I knew you'd understand, Baby Girl. That's what I love about you. Happy one-year."

"You, too."

"You wanna stick around here?"

"No. There's nothing going on here, anyway." I turned to Tomeeka and Keisha who were on the edge of their seats listening. "I'll see you fools later."

Darius and I walked out the door hand-in-hand. One year is a long time for a woman who's never been in love. On the one hand, I felt proud of myself for sticking it out so long, but on the other hand, who the hell was I sticking it out for? It sure the hell wasn't for me.

chapter two

Nothing Comes for Free

"There you go, Tramp," Keisha yelled once I made it in the door.

It was your typical hip-hop, college bash; every pair of legs were grooving to the bass bouncing off the walls and every hand was accompanied by a bottle of some type of alcoholic beverage. And you know I'm not talking about bottles of Chablis or high-priced bubbly. I'm talking about forty-ounce bottles of cheap, malt liquor designed to make people sick or act a fool. Sometimes both.

"This is Connie. She goes to Dry U with us."

I looked behind Keisha and noticed a pretty, cocoa brown sistah standing tall. She was a fierce cross between Lisa Bonet and Nia Long. Her hair was light-brown and hung loosely in naturally, kinky curls passed her shoulders.

"Hey." I extended my right hand. "I'm Kendall."

"Nice to meet you."

We shook and gave each other the sistah stare down from head to toe.

"You seen Tomeeka around here anywhere?" Keisha asked.

"No, I can't hardly see nobody in here." I focused my gaze on Connie. I wondered why I hadn't seen her around campus before.

"It's jumpin', huh?" Keisha yelled.

"What?" I yelled back, snapping back to reality. I couldn't recognize the song but I could tell it was Tupac's voice roaring mightily over the speakers. Tupac was one talented brothah. It's a shame how so many young people fall victim to the false hype of the streets. If you don't agree, sit down and have brunch with Tupac's mother, Afeni.

"Let's go get a drink." Keisha grabbed our hands and led us into the kitchen.

The kitchen seemed to block out some of the noise blaring from the living room. I'm not saying that hip-hop is noise. In fact, I dig hip-hop over that alternative stuff. Although, a little Red Hot Chili Peppers never hurt nobody.

"What the hell is this, Kendall?" Keisha held my right, ring finger up to her face and stared as if she were an appraiser.

"It's nothing. Just a little present." I blushed and snapped my hand out of her grasp.

The night of our anniversary, I could tell by the sneaky look on Darius' face that he was up to something. But I thought he had some roses, a teddy bear or some crap like that. I was in complete shock when he pulled out a black ring box with a half-karat, princess cut, white-gold ring inside. I accepted the gift in embarrassment as I thought about what I presented him just two minutes prior: A pair of white, Chuck Taylor's with a matching white sweatshirt.

"That don't look like no nothin' to me. The only time you get some shit like that is when a brothah's tryin' to tie a sistah down. You ready to be tied, Girl?"

I looked down at the sparkling rock. I guess I was in denial. But couldn't the ring just be a symbol of our relationship as it is now? I mean, a mediocre relationship can be special, too. Don't you think?

"We'll talk about this later." She shook her head and smiled. "Speaking of Darius. Where's he at? Didn't you come together?"

"We came together." I took my drink from Keisha's hand. "But you know how that goes. Boys must play."

"But lucky for us, so must girls. Who wants to be walkin' around with a dude clutterin' up your arm, anyway?"

I looked around. The only "dudes" I saw were the same losers from school. Different races, all drunk and checking out the ladies like we were some type of hunting game fresh in season. But I couldn't really blame them. Most of the women were sporting either skin-tight pants or short-ass skirts that left little to the imagination.

"There you two tramps go."

I looked up and saw Tomeeka. She was dressed like one of the women I described earlier, wearing a thigh-high skirt and halter top. But at least she had the figure to pull it off. Know what I mean?

"Hey, Girl." I leaned forward and gave her a hug. "When'd you get here?"

"Same time as Keisha but I had to call Marcus' ass in the back room."

"I thought he was comin'," Keisha said.

"He was. But you know how he trips about the college scene."

"Yeah," Keisha and I said in unison.

"You remember Connie, don't you, Meeka?"

"Yeah, we had weight training together, last semester. What's up, Connie?"

"It's good to see you, again."

I noticed right away that Connie was an articulate sistah. There wasn't a hint of ghetto slang in her dialect.

"You want somethin' to drink?" Keisha asked Tomeeka.

"Nope. Maybe later."

"Are you sick?"

"Shut the hell up, Keisha. I just don't want none right now."

I cocked my head to the side. Back when I first met Tomeeka, she used to drink damn-near every weekend. Whether we were going out to the club or just hanging out watching a flick at home, she always had a drink in her hand. I wondered what was going on. Hell, maybe she was recognizing the early stages of alcoholism. Who was I to question a good deed?

"Humph." Keisha let out a loud burp. "I don't know what your problem is. But if I was you, I'd get drunk and forget about whatever it is Marcus said or did."

I silently agreed. Minus the "get drunk" part.

"I don't feel like this mess right now, Keisha. You handle business your way and let me handle mine my way."

"Your way? You know Marcus is always bringin' you down. Ain't that right, Kendy?"

I shrugged my shoulders. I didn't want to get in their mess.

Connie raised her eyebrows.

I laughed. "Don't worry. This is an everyday thing. You'll see." I squeezed her right shoulder. I could feel her toned muscles through her shirt. I quickly pulled my hand away. "Those are fly duds, by the way." She had a small, silver hoop-style belly button ring that discreetly peeked beneath her Bob Marley, baby T-shirt.

"You feel me, Kendy?" Tomeeka cut in. She and Keisha were still at it.

I excused myself from Connie, waved a weak, I-ain't-in-this-mess goodbye to Keisha and Tomeeka and walked into the living room to find Darius. I set my drink down on a nearby countertop. The warm liquid was starting to taste bitter as it slid down my throat; that's always been my cue to stop. I mean, why drink something you don't even like just to say you got drunk?

"Hey girl, let's dance."

"Won't you bring that ass this way?"

"Day-am, Babay you look good."

I politely turned down all the pathetic invitations thrown my way. I mean, whatever happened to, "would you like to dance?" I was tired of repeatedly listening to sexual offers disguised as dance invitations. Besides, who wanted to get close to somebody who was all stinky and sweaty? As if it's too much to take a shower and apply some deodorant to those funky underarms. And let's not even begin to discuss the breath factor. Breathing all up in somebody's face with breath that smells like the dead.

"Hey, Kendall. Why is somebody as fine as you standing there by yo'self?"

This is getting old, I thought to myself as I turned down the next sweaty body. I looked around the room for Darius. He was nowhere to be found and I was ready to dance. Who likes to go to a party and just stand around?

"Hey, Kendy," Keisha yelled while dancing with some tall, light-skinned brothah.

I waved. Was I the only one not having fun? I looked around the room and saw Connie standing against the wall. I was about to join her when I saw him: in plain sight was *my* Darius dancing with some pecan-colored broad who was grinding her big butt into him. I was enraged. I know he didn't think I was going to just stand there and let him dance with that freak. You can call me childish but at that moment I decided not to approach Darius. Instead, I decided to get even; I was going to dance with the next fine brothah that stepped my way. I was going to make Darius think twice before ever disrespecting me again.

"Let's dance, Girl." Like clock work, the first body approached me.

I kindly accepted the invitation and immediately started grooving to the beat. From a distance, I could still see Darius occupied in his dance.

"This is the jam, huh?" my unknown partner asked in my right ear. His breath smelled like spearmint gum.

"Yeah, I like this cut," I said, flashing a flirtatious smile. He was kind of cute in a thugged-out sort of way. He was bald-headed and had the same dark, smooth complexion as Tyrese, the model/singer.

"I didn't know you could dance like this, Girl. Back in high school you acted all square and shi-"

"Back in high school?" I stopped dancing. "Do I know you?"

"It's me, Kendall. James. First period Government."

"James? The little boy who use to sit behind me?"

"Yeah, that's me." He opened his jean jacket, exposing his toned abdomen through a white, wife beater. "But I ain't little no more."

I laughed.

"It's good to see you, Kendall."

"You, too."

"Then, don't I get a hug? We're long lost friends, in a way."

I leaned forward and offered him a friendly hug.

He responded with a tight grip on my lower back with his lips dangerously close to my neck. "You smell so good, Girl."

Just as I was about to break away, I felt a heavy hand clutch my arm and swing me around in a one-eighty degree turn. My head and belly remained with James while my body was forced to face it's disruptor.

"What the hell do you think you're doing?"

"Darius, I was just dancing with my friend from high school. It was nothing."

"Bull shit, Kendall. How can you say it was nothing when Dude's hands were all over you? What the hell do you think this is? You think you can just be with me and anybody and everybody else at the same time?"

"It was just a hug-" I interrupted myself, "wait a minute, you were the one getting all freaky over there with that hood rat."

He was speechless.

"Yeah, you thought I didn't see that. I watched the whole thing. How could you disrespect me like that?"

A small crowd started to form around us.

"So in return, you disrespect me? That makes sense. We weren't even dancing that close. Besides, she's my homegirl from church."

"I didn't see nothing religious about the way her ass was all over you."

He had the nerve to smirk.

"You think it's funny?"

"I didn't say that. I just think you're overreactin' a bit."

"Me? You're the one who came over here hollering and embarrassing me in front of my friend James."

"Forget James. You was the one all hugged up with that brothah but I'm the one embarrassing you? Screw that, Kendall. You think this is a game? I didn't buy you that ring to be letting somebody touch on your body. *My* body."

"You better put some more bass in that tone. I don't have time for this shit. I'm out of here." I turned and started to walk away when I felt a hand grab my arm a little tighter than friendly.

"Don't ever walk away from me while I'm talkin' to you."

"Get you hands off me, Darius. That hurts."

Tomeeka and Keisha appeared by my side. Connie stood with her hands folded across her chest.

"Won't you get your hands off my girl." Tomeeka rhythmically moved her head from side-to-side as she spoke.

"Yeah, Mr. Reed don't never put his hands on her so why should you?" Keisha joined in.

Darius immediately let go.

I looked down at my arm. Was I being abused? Was I one of those women I read about but always told myself I'd never become?

"I'm sorry," Darius said to Tomeeka and Keisha.

I was the one with the throbbing arm but he apologized to them.

"It's cool, everybody. Show's over," I said to the handful of people who were still watching. "I need some air." I walked out the front door.

Keisha and Tomeeka followed me.

"What happened?" Tomeeka asked.

"Yeah, Kendy. What happened?"

Surprisingly, I found my voice. I mumbled out the entire story starting with me catching Darius dancing with that freak and ending with me hugging James. I looked down at my arm. It was still red but the throbbing had begun to subside.

"Fine-ass James?" Keisha asked, smiling.

"Bald-headed, chocolate-kiss James?" Tomeeka added.

"Shut-up." I forced a smile.

"Who was that hoodie dancin' all up in Darius' face?" Tomeeka asked.

For those of you who don't know, a "hoodie" is common term for a "hood rat" or a nasty female from the ghetto. If you don't know what I'm talking about, just turn your television to BET and you'll see plenty of "hoodies" shaking their computer-altered behinds.

"I think it was Sheronda from the south," I said.

"Herpes mouth, Sheronda?" Tomeeka asked.

"I think so."

"Don't trip, Girl. I'll school her, later."

"No, don't do that, Keisha. It ain't worth it. Besides, it ain't her fault."

"Has he ever gotten mad like that before?" Tomeeka asked.

"Not that I can remember. He's always been overprotective but not violent. Maybe it's because of this damn ring."

"What ring?" Tomeeka asked.

I held up my ring finger.

"Shit, Kendall. You in over your head. You love him?"

I sighed.

"Maybe this ain't the time for you to answer that, huh?"

"What you think, Meeka? That was inappropriate. Have some tact."

"Shut-up, Keisha. Don't start with me. This ain't the time or place for mess."

"Yeah, I have enough mess of my own," I said. "I'll be okay, though. You two go back in the party."

"You sure?"

"Yeah, Keisha. Go back in before your man finds somebody else." I laughed weakly.

"Hell no, Kendy. We goin' right now. Keisha can do whatever she wants but we leavin'." Tomeeka saw right through my jive ass like glass.

"Maybe that fine-ass Derrick'll drive me home. In the morning." Keisha stood up.

"Tramp," Tomeeka said.

"Call me, Kendy." Keisha disappeared into the house.

"Kendall, can I talk to you?" Darius stumbled up to me. An all too familiar scent of alcohol pierced my nostrils.

"You're drunk. Talk to me later when you sober up."

"I'm not drunk. I only had one, two, maybe three drinks."

"Get away from me, please."

"Just listen to me, Kendall. I'll be real quick."

"She said she don't wanna talk to you right now. Habla Ingles?"

"Tomeeka, can you please get into some business of your own?" Darius had the nerve to yell.

"It's one thing to treat me like shit but now you're involving my friends. Get out of my face. There's nothing I wanna hear from you. And if you keep this up, I might not ever talk to you again."

"Kendall, if you would just listen for a minute."

"Go, Darius," I said, then walked off. At that moment, I wanted nothing more than to get into the car and drive away forever. I wanted to run from Darius' drunk ass. There was only one problem: where was I going?

chapter three

Wounded Bird

It was nearly 4 A.M. when I crept in the door. The familiar scent of berry potpourri greeted me as I tiptoed through the house. Up until the moment the pleasant scent hit my nostrils, I felt alone and scared. It was as if the very world that I knew as my own was crumbling before my eyes.

I walked directly to my room and stripped down to panties and a T-shirt. My entire body was sticky with sweat and my throat felt dry. My throat was craving the smooth taste of chocolate, soy milk. But when I opened the refrigerator door, my mood shifted from pissed-off to down-right irate; there was a forty ounce of beer blocking the soy milk. Daddy could at least have the common courtesy to hide his beer on the back shelf of the refrigerator. I mean, what if my younger cousins were to open the door and see that shit? Kids see enough of that crap on television commercials. Know what I mean? The things you have sitting in the front of the refrigerator are usually the highest on your priority list. Was beer more vital to Daddy than natural sustenance i.e. food and water?

I thought of going to my room to relieve myself of the built-up rage that was on the verge of causing an explosion. But what good would that do? When I finished writing, I'd only get thirsty again and restart the rage that the writing tamed. What the hell. The cycle had to be broken somehow. And at ninety-dollars-an-hour, Dr. Porsche had to know something. Don't you think?

Dear Reader,

I remember when I was a Blue Jay. No, I'm not trying to be metaphoric nor am I confessing any beliefs in reincarnation. I'm talking about the seven-year-old version of girl scouts: the sexist alternative to Boy Scouts. Since Mother didn't want me sitting around some campfire, clutching a Swiss Army Knife with a bunch of little boys, I was forced to learn how to sew with a bunch of pink-wearing, giggling girls. But after a few months, I actually started to enjoy the once-a-week sessions in my elementary school cafeteria. I learned how to crochet', bake a cake and play tennis. I enjoyed the innocent physical contact between me and my fellow Blue Jays. A sisterhood had began to form that exceeded the distant relationship between Kiara and me. So, when my first camp-out was announced, I was more than excited to run home and tell my parents.

Mother volunteered to be a chaperone. On the night of the trip, we had our sleeping bags and overnight suitcase waiting by the door. The instant Daddy came home from work, we were going to meet the rest of the Blue Jays at Dryton National Park. But Daddy was late coming home. Mother tried to call one of the other mother's to pick us up, but since it was before the age of cellular phones, she was unsuccessful in her attempts. Mother was worried but I knew that my Daddy would not let his Baby Girl down. I knew that any moment Daddy would walk through that door with his arms opened wide. I waited patiently by the door. Seconds turned to minutes. Minutes turned to hours. Still, I waited. But the door never opened.

Later that night, I remember crying myself to sleep in Mother's arms. It was the first time my father broke my heart. And the next morning when I saw him passed out on the couch with a beer can by his side, I knew it wouldn't be the last time.

Kendall Renee Reed

chapter four

Another Statistic

Saturday morning I woke up feeling like fifty insects were simultaneously nibbling at the right side of my brain. My headache wasn't due to alcohol consumption; my headache was due to being awake all night with anger and frustration. I mean, who did Darius think he was grabbing on me like that? He's lucky I'm a woman of tact and didn't punch him in the face right on the spot. But I hate to be the one to ruin the party. You know the person that everybody leaves talking about and shaking their heads saying, "*She* always has to mess stuff up," or, "We were having fun until *they* started fighting." I've always vowed never to be the *she* or *they* being referred to.

I looked down at my arm. I was relieved to see there was no bruise forming. I'm usually the type to bruise if I brush up against something remotely hard. Even though there was no *physical* bruise to mark what happened, there was a bruise forming that would take even longer to go away; there was a bruise on my pride. Even though I've never loved Darius, it still hurts to be treated any less than the best. Know what I mean?

I slid on a pair of cotton shorts and a tank-top and walked down the hallway into the kitchen. Mother was cooking oatmeal on the stove.

"Morning," I said with sleep heavily drenched in my voice.

"Morning? It's almost one," Mother said.

"I had a long night." I stretched and yawned.

"I know. I waited up for you until two."

I laughed. Ever since I can remember, Mother has always waited up for me. When I arrived home from my first date, she was right on the couch ready to hear all the "innocent" details. At five-in-the-morning, when I arrived home from my senior prom, guess who was asleep on the couch? I don't mind, though. It's just one of those things that make her, "Mother." Know what I mean?

"How was the party?" Mother added milk and sugar to her oatmeal.

"Hey, not so much sugar. Did you take your insulin?" I dodged her question.

"Yeah, Dr. Kendall. I took my insulin fifteen minutes ago like I'm supposed to."

"Tell *me* something."

"My sugar was one-twenty this morning. I've been doing good."

I opened the refrigerator to get some chocolate soymilk but Mother's reduced-fat milk was blocking it. I was relieved that the beer was no longer in the way. I poured myself a glassful and gulped away, allowing it to spill from the corners of my lips.

"Kendy, I don't see how you can drink that stuff. That's why you all skin and bones."

"Mother, I'm not that skinny. I'm actually five pounds over my weight limit."

"Okay, okay." She sat down at the table. "You going to the barbecue, later?"

"Barbecue?" I reached for an overripe banana. "What barbecue?"

"Spence's birthday party. You do still remember Spence, don't you? Your favorite cousin?"

"Oh, shi-," I caught myself. "I mean, I almost forgot."

"Kendy?" Mother sang. "Don't make me get my belt."

"Sorry." I laughed. "I'm tired, today. I'll send my present with you." I laughed, again. "After I go buy it."

"You somethin' else." Mother laughed. "I'll pick him up somethin' for you. What about that new roller coaster game for his computer?"

"Sounds good."

I walked into the living room to watch TV but Daddy had already beaten me to it. He was watching a basketball game and reading the newspaper. The King's were holding down the court.

"Morning, Daddy."

"Morning, Kendall."

"Who's playing?"

"The King's. And they kickin' the Laker's butts, too."

"Yeah? What's the score?"

"Eighty-six to seventy-one. Webber is puttin' it on 'em."

Daddy was excited because I was interested in his game. And believe me when I say *his* game. Daddy relives his days of high school stardom through professional sports. When Chris Webber suspends in midair with three seconds left on the clock to score the winning point from damn-near mid court, Daddy visualizes himself getting the glory. From what I've been told, Daddy was a great athlete. He was a basketball star in high school and he ran cross country like nobody's business. You're probably wondering why Thomas Reed isn't playing side-by-side with Webber, Bibby and Jackson. Just ask the jealous point guard from the opposing Dryton High team that clipped young Thomas during a routine lay-up his junior year. As Daddy explained it, his entire life came crashing down before his eyes as he lay in the hospital bed after his knee surgery. I can't imagine how he must've felt when the surgeon told him he could never play basketball or run again.

"Money." Daddy rose to his feet and yelled. "Now that's what I'm talkin' about. In your face, Shaq."

"What happened?" Mother yelled from the dining room.

"Webber hit another three," I answered.

"No, he didn't just hit another three. He rose over they heads and dropped the ball in the hoop." Daddy demonstrated with a dramatic imitation. "Swoosh."

I laughed. Daddy should've at least been a coach or something. If he can't physically be running up and down that court, he should at least be on the sideline yelling out orders. Know what I mean?

I stood up and walked towards my room. I placed the remaining bite of my squishy banana in my mouth and tossed the peel into the garbage can.

"Kendall, throw this away for me while you're in there."

I looked back to see what Daddy was talking about. That's when the irritation returned; in his hand was the forty-ounce bottle that was blocking the soymilk, the previous night. Why couldn't Daddy and I have just one conversation, just one moment when he wasn't already full of alcohol?

"Dammit," I cursed silently under my breath as I grabbed the empty bottle and tossed it into the garbage can.

Before my shower, I laid down on my bed and stared at the ceiling. The glow-in-the-dark, galaxy stickers were starting to peel. I bought the stars with my first, paper route check when I was twelve-years-old. Seven years later, I was still laying in the same bed. Hair longer, breasts slightly larger but still staring at the same tired-ass stars. Somebody was trying to tell me something. Don't you think?

* * *

"Wake up, Kendall."

"What time is it?" I sat up in my bed. The sun had already made it's departure.

"Eight," Mother said.

"Eight? I been sleep all day?" I clicked on the lamp and glanced at my watch.

"You must've been tired."

"I must've. How was the barbecue?"

"Same old, same old. I can give you details later. Tomeeka's here. You want me to send her back?"

"Tomeeka? What's she doing here? Yeah, yeah. Send her on back." I slipped on my pink, fuzzy slippers.

"Come on back, Tomeeka." Mother disappeared into the living room.

"Hey, Kendy." Tomeeka walked in and sat down on the edge of the bed. Her eyes were swollen and her hair was disheveled.

"Hey, Meeka. What's wrong?"

"I need to talk to somebody. And you the most reliable friend I got."

"Talk to me. You know you can tell me anything."

"What I'm about to tell you, I haven't told nobody. Not even my mama."

I leaned forward.

"You know how Marcus was locked up for a few months?"

"For the car-jacking incident?"

"He got out two months ago, right?"

"Yeah." I hate tap dancing unless it's done by Sammy. Know what I mean?

"You know how they get when they get out?"

"No." I mean, how am I to know about post-prison behavior?

"Come on, Kendall. Don't make me come out and say it."

"Say what?"

"Damn, Kendy. You really are a virgin, aren't you?"

"Get to the point. This is about you, not me."

"Okay, okay. Cool out, I'll tell you."

I rolled my eyes.

"When a dude get out he ain't had none in awhile."

"Okay, I get it now. That's nasty."

"You wanted to know." She smiled.

"Go on."

"When he got out, he wanted it all the time." Her eyes filled with tears. "Like every damn minute."

I gently placed my hand on her shoulder. "He didn't force you, again. Did he?"

"No, I wanted to, this time." She blushed. "I was willing."

"Tell *me* something."

"Anyway, we was doin' it all the time. Everywhere, too. At his mama's house, in the apartment, in the car, in the bathroom stall while a kid watched."

"Too much info."

"One night, well a few times, he didn't have no protection. But it was good and you know how dudes get when you try to stop."

I rolled my eyes, again.

"Sorry. I guess you don't know. But I made sure he pulled out in time."

"Pulled out? Do you know how careless that is?" I waved my hands in the air. "Besides being filthy, that's dangerous, Meeka. You don't know where Marcus has stuck that thing."

"I know. I know it was stupid. But now what can I do. I'm about to be a mama."

"A what?"

"I'm pregnant." She laid her head down on my shoulder and sobbed.

I hugged her tight and after about five minutes, I said, "What you gonna do?"

She stopped crying and sat up. "I don't know. But I know I'ma keep it. I ain't down with abortions."

"No doubt. I didn't mean abortion. I just meant with school and stuff. I mean, does Marcus know?"

"No, I ain't told him, yet." You're the only person who knows." She wiped her nose with the back of her hand.

"Only me? Not even Keisha?" I handed her a tissue from my nightstand.

She blew her nose. "Especially not Keisha. I gotta keep this on the hush. I can't have it gettin' all around. You know how people be talkin'?"

"Yeah, I know. When you gonna tell him?"

"Who? Marcus?"

I nodded my head.

"This weekend when we get together."

"How you think he's gonna react?"

"You know how Marcus is. He damn-near tried to kill me when I asked if he had any kids. Fractured my arm in two places."

"That's a damn shame. *Does* he have kids?"

"Yeah, he got a two-year old son from some old broad he used to live with on the north side."

"That's a trip. Why do you put up with his shit?"

"Cause I love him. You should understand that. It's kind of like what went down last night at the party. How's your arm, by the way?"

I was furious. How dare she compare Darius to Marcus? "That's not the same and you know it. Marcus broke your arm. Darius only grabbed me. How the hell is that the same?"

"Abuse is abuse, Kendy. Whether you like it or not. The first time Marcus put his hands on me, it was a grab. The next time, it was a push. Before I knew it, he was punching the shit out of me."

I hung my head down. Darius would never hit me. Would he?

"Sorry, I'm just on edge. That was uncalled for. I didn't mean to bring up last night."

"That's okay. It's how you felt."

"I just don't know what to do. But I do know welfare is out of the question. Screw that. I ain't tryin' to be another statistic."

"I know what you mean. Another single mom on welfare."

"Yeah, my mom went through that shit. My aunties. I don't wanna be like that. I wanna be legit."

"You staying in school? You know professional black adults are on the endangered list."

"I'm goin' part time when I get closer to deliverin'. It'll take me longer but I'll manage."

I nodded. I was scared for her. I mean, raising a child, working and going to school was going to be hard.

"My OB/GYN said she'd give me a job cleaning up and stocking stuff in her clinic after I deliver. I been interested in nursing."

"I didn't know that? How long you been interested in that?"

"I been interested in medicine since I was little but I ain't feelin' eight years of school."

"School ain't for everybody."

"You think he's gonna leave me when he finds out?"

"Marcus?" I played dumb to avoid answering the obvious.

"Yeah. You think he'll support the baby?"

"I don't know, Meeka. I hope so," I answered although deep inside I knew that Marcus' departure would be the safest antidote to Tomeeka's dilemma.

"I don't know what I'ma do if he leaves me. I'm scared."

I held her hand tightly. "I know it's scary but you know what?"

"What?"

"I'll support you one-hundred percent. Whatever you need, just ask. I'm here for you every step of the way."

"Thanks, Kendy. I knew I could count on you." She leaned forward and hugged me.

I could feel her body trembling as I held her. Sympathetically, I could feel her pain radiating throughout my body. And at that moment all my problems felt obsolete. For once in my life, I felt completely helpless.

chapter five

American Sweet-Potato Pie

"Baby, I uh. I mean, you know I didn't mean to-"

I stood there with my arms folded in the classic, I-ain't-trying-to-hear-this-shit position. The body language was all there: rolled eyes, balled fists, head turned. Darius knew he was in hot water after I hung up in his face when he had the nerve to call me, Sunday night. He called back three times trying to apologize but I wasn't trying to hear it. So, it was giving me great pleasure seeing him grovel in the main quad area at Dryton State on a busy Monday morning.

"I guess I had too much to drink. I didn't know what I was doing."

Blame it on the alcohol. I shook my head and rolled my eyes as he spoke. My silver-rimmed shades rested on the tip of my nose.

"I'm not sayin' I'm not responsible for my own actions. 'Cause I am. I never should've put my hands on you. It was stupid."

"You got that right."

"I'll never do it, again. I'm so sorry."

I rolled my eyes.

"Please, please, Baby, forgive me. I'll die if you leave me. I need you."

He was making me sick.

"I know I messed up. I really screwed things up. I wouldn't be in school if it wasn't for you. If it wasn't for you, I'd probably be on the streets sellin' crack to my own mama."

My face softened.

"Please give me another chance. I even wrote you a poem."

I smiled involuntarily.

He pulled a crumpled piece of binder paper from the pocket of his khakis and started to read. "*I never knew it could be like this. I never hardly tried. It's your smile that I'm gonna miss. Please don't make me cry. If you tell me it's over, what will I do then? You bring me luck like a clover. You without me is a sin. Kendall, Kendall, give me one more chance-"*

I laughed. I had to admit, he did look kind of cute standing there reading that awful poem in front of his peers. He was sacrificing his "tough guy" image just to please me. I felt flattered, in a way. Nobody had written me poetry before. I decided to give in. "Okay, I accept your apology."

"You do?" He looked like a kitten begging for milk.

"Yeah I do. But you better not ever put your hands on me, again. I mean it, Darius."

"I promise." He answered as if he'd just won the million-dollar prize

"Now come give me a hug." I smiled.

"I missed you, Baby Girl." He pulled me close, by my waist.

"You better have missed me, Mr. Poet."

"You didn't like my poem?"

I grinned.

"I worked all night on that."

"Well, in that case, I loved it." I linked my arm through his. "Now take your girl to breakfast."

"What about chemistry?"

"I think we have enough chemistry right here." I leaned forward and pecked him on the cheek.

He turned my face and kissed my lips.

We headed toward the parking lot.

* * *

"I'm never eating, again."

"Me neither." I unbuttoned the top button to my light-blue jeans.

Darius burped loudly. It reeked of maple syrup.

After an apology breakfast followed by a kiss-ass trip to the mall, Darius and I decided to recuperate at his house. We were laying side-by-side on his queen-sized bed so stuffed and tired we could hardly move.

"What time do you have to be back?" He slid his left arm around my neck.

"I have literature at two."

"Cool. That gives us two hours to rest. I hardly got any sleep last night." His thumb moved slowly up and down my shoulder.

"Why couldn't you sleep?"

"Well, obviously because of what I did to you. But also because I had to take Ms. Super Bitch to Value Smart at midnight."

The Bitch he was referring to was his step-mom. Normally I don't condone a woman being called a bitch. I mean, don't we hear enough of that in music? But Darius' step-mom, Helen, puts the 'b' in bitch. Every word that comes out of that woman's mouth is selfish and downright hateful. And the control she has over Darius' pops is unbelievable. Can you spell P-whipped? I swear that woman has a voodoo spell placed on Mr. Mayfield.

"At midnight? What the hell did she possibly need at midnight that couldn't wait until morning? Why couldn't your dad take her?"

"Calm down. Pops car is messed up, remember? And you know I don't let nobody but you drive my truck."

"But she couldn't wait until morning?"

"It was a female problem, I think. She ran out of tampons."

"It's still not your responsibility."

"I know. But she does makes Pops smile. Moms ain't never done that. You know?"

I nodded.

"Speaking of my moms." He rolled over onto his left side to face me. He placed his right hand across my stomach. "I saw her yesterday at Grandma's house. She looks real bad, Baby. Real bad. I think she's shootin' up."

"What makes you say that?" I rolled over onto my side to face him.

"She's actin' different. More calm than before. And you know how crack makes people all jittery and shit?"

I nodded.

"Yesterday she was sittin' on the couch in front of the TV, noddin' off. And the TV wasn't even on."

"Damn, Darius. I'm sorry." I averted my eyes to the black comforter on the bed.

"I just wanna strangle her sometimes. Why would she do that to herself? To me? To her family? She don't care about nobody but herself."

"Darius, she can't care about anybody. Drugs are her life, right now. You can't take it personal."

"Can't take it personal? She's my mom, ain't that personal enough? Doesn't she realize that I'm her life, too?" He sat up.

"I know. Hey, I'm on your side. All I'm saying is don't give up on her. That's all you can do."

"I know." He laid back down beside me. "I wasn't yelling at you. You know that, don't you."

"Of course, I know. I can't imagine how you must feel." I laid down on his chest. He stroked my hair, gently.

I started to drift off to sleep.

"Kendall?" Darius interrupted my preliminary slumber.

"Huh?" I answered with my eyes still closed.

"I love you. You know that, don't you?"

"Yeah, I know."

"No, I really mean that. I've never loved nobody the way I love you."

I smiled uneasily. It sounded like a speech I'd heard before from my first boyfriend Nate. Then again with Kenny. And the saga continues.

"I didn't give you that ring just 'cause we been together a year. I gave you that ring 'cause you're the one. I'm gonna marry you, Baby Girl. As soon as I get my shit together."

I held my breath. Marriage? Who said I wanted to get married? And if I did, who said it was going to be to Darius?

"I just can't right now. I work four days a week makin' them damn pizzas and I still don't make enough to move out of Pops' house. I wanna give you the world. And I will, someday. That I can promise. That's what this ring means." He climbed on top of me. His face was only inches from mine. "Baby, I promise to marry you."

I frowned. How the hell could he promise to do something I never requested? I'm not planning on getting married any time soon. I mean, when I get married, I want to be in love. I want to experience the same feelings I read about so often in literature books. I want to be able to look that person in the eyes and know deep down that I want to spend the rest of my life with them. And until then, I, Kendall Renee' Reed, shall remain single. I looked down at my ring. What had I gotten myself into?

"You hear me, Baby Girl? I want to marry you."

"That's sweet."

"Sweet?"

"I mean, thank you." I tried to sound humble but marriage isn't something to play around with.

"Okay." He kissed me gently, "I guess I put a lot on your plate. No need to respond now. I know how you feel about me."

I managed a weak smile.

He started to kiss me. Slowly at first, then more passionately as the seconds rolled by.

I kissed him back lazily with my mind still fixated on the marriage proposition. And as he continued to kiss me, I started to think about my future:

Will I be successful? Will I get a piece of the American sweet potato pie and be all that I can be? Will I live in a house, in the country with a long-haired Chihuahua named Pancho with a little turtle pond in the back? Will I be accepting the Pulitzer Prize for writing the greatest African-Amerikan novel?

Darius cupped my face in his hands and began to kiss my entire face.

Will I have a Kendall II? Will I wait on the couch for her to come home from her first date? Will I be the mom that Mother is to me?

"Oh, Kendall," he murmured as he kissed my ear.

Will I be alone?

He kissed my neck.

Will I be lonely?

His tongue traced a path to my right shoulder.

Will I be happy?

That's when I started to tune in to what was happening. I wasn't happy with myself at that moment. It's not fair to me or to Darius to pretend that the love is there when, in cold reality, even the like is gone.

"Would you look at that? It's quarter to two." I slid from beneath his body.

He laid back on the bed and sighed.

I pulled on my red, button-up shirt over my white, wife-beater.

"You have gots to be kidding." He made a lewd gesture towards his crotch. "You're gonna just leave me like this? Again?"

"Let's not start this, Darius. You knew I had class."

He stood up and slipped on his white, hooded sweatshirt. "I'm sick of this."

"So what are you saying?"

"Forget it. Let's just go." He put on his White Sox cap and walked out the door.

I followed silently with feelings of anger and guilt swarming through me.

They say love is a two way street. Then why was I trapped on an abandoned dirt road?

chapter six

Deep Wounds Never Mend

"Tell me about your ankle."

"What about it?"

"I want to discuss what you said earlier about falling off your bunk bed when you were fourteen."

"Since I'm paying, shouldn't it be about what I wanna talk about?"

"Of course, Kendall. But since you brought it up, I want to talk more about it. You're paying me to help you, right?"

"Yeah. But talking about old shit from the past doesn't help me. I mean, most kids break bones don't they?"

"Yes, that's true. But you did it intentionally and that's serious. Self-inflicted harm is nothing to take lightly."

I rolled my eyes. I wasn't intentionally trying to be mean. I guess I was just having one of those someone-pissed-in-my-cornflakes kind of days. You know the kind of day where the instant you open your eyes you start to wish you could close them and sleep the day away? Or maybe that's just me.

"Kendall, I need to ask you a serious question."

My hands were clasped together tightly on my lap.

"Was that the only time you ever tried to hurt yourself?"

"It was an accident." I didn't want to be forced to discuss every single time I've physically hurt myself. Besides, it's not like I've ever tried to commit suicide. Know what I mean?

"You didn't really answer my question. But if it makes you feel uncomfortable, I'll leave it alone for now." Dr. Porsche leaned back in her chair dejectedly.

I sighed. "I think I have my thong on backwards, today."

She laughed.

"I'm sorry."

"That's the Kendall I know."

"I don't know why I did it. Maybe I was angry."

"At who?"

"Everybody, I guess. I was at a breakdown point, so to speak. School was kicking my ass. My friends were getting on my last nerves. And my boyfriend, Nate, wasn't giving me any room to breathe."

Dr. Porsche sat back in her chair.

"I don't remember if it was Saturday or Sunday. I do know it was a weekend because the morning after the incident, Nate and I were supposed to go to Six Flags. But I was tired of having a boyfriend. I wanted to just be fourteen and hang out with my friends at the mall or something. I didn't want to be in a relationship and be part of a 'we' when I wasn't even sure about the 'I'. Understand what I mean?"

"Perfectly, Kendall. Well said."

"Anyway, it was late at night. Even the house was sleep. I had a lot on my mind, so I just sat up on the top of my bunk bed."

Dr. Porsche remained quiet, writing occasionally.

"Like I mentioned earlier, Nate and I were supposed to go to Six Flags but I didn't want to go. So I came up with the only solution my fourteen-year-old mind could create." I absently picked at a mosquito bite on my right forearm. It started to bleed.

Dr. Porsche reached into her desk and handed me a band-aid.

"I jumped off the bunk bed, as hard as I could, onto my ankle. But the impact of the fall didn't do anything to harm me so I grabbed my steel softball bat." I shifted my eyes to the ground. "It took at least ten blows to finish the job."

"That's awful, Kendall. Did your mom know?"

"No, she just thought I fell."

"Was that the first time you hurt yourself?"

"The first and last. But I can't say I never thought about it."

"And now?"

"Well every once in awhile, when it feels like life is weighing me down, I get the urge to hurt myself. Like to maybe get some time off work."

"Can I ask you a question?"

"Yeah."

"Why do you think about hurting yourself?"

"I guess I get so fed up and angry that I wanna scream."

"Then why don't you scream?"

"People would think I'm crazy."

"As opposed to breaking your own bones?"

"But I've only hurt myself once."

"Physically once. But you hurt yourself emotionally every time you even think of harming yourself."

I sighed in defeat.

"One more question?"

"Okay."

"What usually triggers these self-destructive thoughts?"

"Anger. I told you that."

"Anger is a secondary emotion. Meaning, it only occurs after another emotion is present. Hurt, guilt, sadness. There's always another emotion lingering behind anger."

"Many things trigger my anger."

"Like?"

"Like when I was younger, I used to imagine being injured to get Daddy's attention. He's always worked a lot and the times he *was* home, he spent in his room."

"You'd want to be injured so he could stay home from work?"

"Yeah. But that was when I was younger."

"Now?"

"Now I get enraged when I'm knee deep in crap. Like when I'm in a dead-end, one-sided relationship because I don't wanna be alone. Or when I'm stuck doing a job I have no desire to do."

"Like working at the lab?"

I nodded. "And every time I see Daddy take a drink of alcohol." I shuddered. "It kills me."

Dr. Porsche sat back in her chair silently, looking me dead in the eyes.

I allowed my eyes to flutter downward, focusing on my band-aid.

"Your father. He likes to read a lot, right?"

"He reads the newspaper every morning. Why?"

"I want you to try this:"

I leaned forward in my chair.

"Start writing a letter to your father."

"A letter?"

"Yes. Write him a letter telling him exactly what's on your mind. Pretend like you're talking to me, but write it down. Use a pen so you can't erase and write everything that comes to mind."

"But what if I hurt him? Some of the shit in my mind would probably make him upset."

"Write it, anyway. It's good for you to make him upset. Emotions are powerful. Maybe your anger might get him to start thinking about his actions. Maybe he'll realize how much he's hurt you. And then, maybe you can release some of that pinned up anger you're harvesting. Turning your anger inward only causes more damage." She took a deep breath. "You know what the most powerful emotion is?"

"What?"

"Love," she answered in a calm voice.

"Love?" I asked. Would I ever escape that awkward word? I mean, was there a giant billboard with my picture posted in Times Square that said, "This girl has never been in love. Please rub it in her face?"

"Kendall, it sounds like your father loves you a lot. I'm sure if he knew how much his drinking is affecting you, he'd reconsider getting help."

"You may be right, Dr. Porsche."

"I sure hope so, Kendall. I sure hope so."

chapter seven

Ms. Doubtfire

"Let me see it, again."

I was sitting up at my sister, Kiara's, two-story, four-bedroom house overlooking the entire Bay Area. It was Saturday afternoon and my boss let me off work early because business was slow. The view of the mountains were beautiful, especially after coming from the flat desert plains of Dryton Valley.

"See." I held out my ring for the millionth time.

"Damn, Ken. It took Tim eight years to get me a ring."

"Get out of here. Look at the size of this house. Me and Darius still live with our mama's." I laughed. "And that ring on your finger ain't exactly tiny," I said, referring to the one-karat diamond ring Kiara sported on her finger.

"Yeah, but it don't come easy. Our mortgage payment is ridiculous out here. I work at that damn law office ten hours a day. And Tim's at his practice doin' root canals damn-near six days a week. We barely see each other." Kiara pulled her microscopic braids back into a ponytail.

Kiara changes hairstyle like draws. One day her hair is long, the next it's short. One day it's jet-black, the next day it's blond. Then curly. Then straight. Sometimes I want to say, "Damn, Ki, make up your mind." But she always looks too good to say anything negative. The girl can work the hell out of some hair. She should be in some Beverly Hills hair shop with clients like Mary J. Blige and Halle Berry sitting up in her chair. But, who knows, maybe accounting is her passion.

"At least you both like what you do. And you love each other so much it probably makes up for all the work. Plus, when you do decide to have kids, they'll live a comfortable life. And I'm not saying that comfortable equals money." I glanced over at

Kiara. People always say we look alike with our butterscotch complexions and flat noses. Except, Kiara is thick and shapely with ass and hips to spare.

"I know what you mean, Ken. My kids won't have to want for nothing. I want them to live in a stable environment."

"A mentally stable household *is* important." I left the window and joined Kiara at the cherry oak round table.

"Very important." She paused and stared at the white ceiling fan above us.

I squirmed uncomfortably in my seat. I hoped the conversation wouldn't steer into the wrong direction: a.k.a to the life of the Reed family. I'm not trying to say that I led an awful life of constant struggle. And I'm also not trying to say that I'm not one-hundred and twenty percent grateful for everything my parents gave us, both physically and mentally. But I do have to admit, we had some trying times.

"Anyway." Kiara was the first to break the silence.

"Yeah, anyway." I sighed.

She smiled at me, sneakily.

I smiled back knowing exactly what that sneaky smile meant; Kiara was about to get nosy.

"You tryin' to call yourself engaged now?"

"No. It's just an anniversary ring."

"Does *he* know that?"

"Yeah, of course he knows." I tugged on the neckline of my shirt. "It's getting hot in here. Can we open a window?"

"You sure he don't know?"

"Of course I'm sure. I'm not getting married no time soon."

"Okay. I'll drop it for now."

I sighed in relief.

"For now." She stood up and clapped her hands. "Let's go to 'The City.' There's a Spanish restaurant I want you to try."

"You know I hate greasy Mexican food, Ki."

"Not Mexican food, Idiot. Spanish food."

"What's the difference?"

"There's a lot more seafood and pasta in Spanish food. Besides, Spain and Mexico are two different places." She laughed, loudly.

I flipped her off.

"It's less fattening. Not that your little skinny ass couldn't stand a little fat."

"I'm not that skinny." I absently ran my hand over my belly. It was caved in a bit and I could feel my ribs underneath my breasts. I'll bet I looked sickening.

"Not that skinny? You not foolin' anyone by wearin' those baggy dips all the time."

I laughed. I guess my baggy, royal blue cotton sweat suit couldn't hide my weight no matter how hard I tried. Hell, I was born skinny. What's a girl to do?

* * *

"Once again, you were right, Sis. This is good."

"I told you it'd be good, *Ms. Doubtfire*."

I laughed. "You know how I am about putting stuff in my mouth I don't know nothing about."

"Yeah, I know." She playfully rolled her eyes. "That's why you still a virgin."

I laughed harder then gave her the bird.

We were sitting up at a quaint Spanish restaurant in downtown San Francisco, sipping on cold margaritas and munching on warm plates of food. Even though a cool, Bay breeze was blowing outside, it was still stuffy in the packed non-air conditioned restaurant. I swear there were at least thirty people seated wall-to-wall in the five-hundred square foot space. But despite it's stuffiness, the cooks could get down in the kitchen. I mean, do you honestly think people would be crammed up in an uncomfortably hot space for nasty-ass food? The food was unbelievable. I was working on a seafood, pasta medley with grilled shrimp, clams, baby lobster, scallops and eel topped with a lemon-wine and herb sauce. Kiara was working on a fried potato platter, topped with melted cheese, chicken and some type of exotic black mushroom.

"Speaking of virgins," Kiara continued between slurps, "you still are one, right?"

I frowned. I wonder why people felt the need to get in my business. As if I was carrying a sign that said something like, "My business is your business. Please get in it." Know what I mean?

"Well?"

"Ki, you know I hate talking about this. So please."

"Please nothing." She popped a cheese-drenched potato into her mouth. "I just wanna know what my sister is about. Is that a crime?"

"No."

"No what?" She leaned forward. "No you're not a virgin or no it's not a crime?"

I laughed. "No, it's not a crime and yes, I'm still a virgin."

"The last American virgin." She laughed. "Just make sure you don't get married before taking a test drive."

"What?"

"What if you get married and find out on your honeymoon that he's a midget." She held up her pinky finger.

I cracked up. "You're crazy. Can we talk about something else? You know how uncomfortable this makes me?"

"Don't be uncomfortable. We're family."

"I know. I'm just not comfortable with the fact that I've never-" I hesitated. "I've never even wanted to. You know?"

"You mean, you're scared?"

"No, it's not that. I mean, I've never gotten to the point where I wanted to."

"You never let anybody get far, you mean?"

I focused on a broken down ceiling fan above my head trying to think of a better way to explain what I was trying to say. I mean, how can you properly tell a person you've never been turned on by a guy?

"Talk to me, Ken."

"I guess what I'm trying to say is, I've never felt the desire to even try. You know?" I could feel my face turning red.

"You're scared, then?"

"No. My mind just shuts off. I think of other things. You know?"

"Hmm." She twisted her lips sideways, then sucked her teeth. "Have you ever tried to take things further? I mean, how far have you gotten?"

"Far enough, I guess. First base, maybe second once or twice."

"Can I ask you a question?"

"Depends on what it is."

"Have you ever been hurt?"

"Yeah. But I mean, everybody gets hurt at least once."

She took a sip of her margarita. "No, not that kind of hurt. I mean, physically hurt."

"Like hit?" My mind reverted back to Darius.

"Like forced to-"

"No," I interrupted her, "of course not. I'd have told you something like that."

"Whew." She sighed with relief. "Now that's out of the way. Let's move on."

"Good, I hate talking about this, anyway."

"Oh, no you don't. I wanna know why you're still a virgin. You don't trust Darius?"

"I don't know. I just haven't felt that spark with anybody." I played with my half-full plate.

"Okay. But can I ask you another personal question?"

"Damn, Ki. How much more personal can this get?"

"We've only scratched the surface."

I laughed uneasily.

"Have you ever felt," she lowered her voice, "you know?"

I coughed and looked around the room wondering if anybody heard her. "I'm not even answering that."

"Fair enough. I just asked because I think lust is important in a relationship."

"What about love?"

"Lust comes first."

I looked down at my plate.

"I wasn't trying to make you feel bad. In fact, I admire the fact that you're waiting. I wish I had waited. I mean, with Rick and I, the lust was there but the love never showed up. Unfortunately, I never tried to stop it from going passed a kiss."

"Rick? Back when you were sixteen?"

"Yeah. I wish I'd waited because I definitely wasn't ready for all the responsibility that came along with it all. So, I'm proud that you waited so long, Ken." She smiled at me. "But I do hope that someday you're able to feel the way

I feel every time Tim and I kiss. The point where the love meets the lust halfway."

"It'll happen."

"I know. Someday, it will. And whoever that person is, don't ever be ashamed to let those feelings happen. Male or female, I'll support you one-hundred percent."

I raised my right eyebrow. Male or female? Did my sister think I was gay? I mean, I would never deny my feelings if they ever happened to lean towards a woman. But, never have I even insinuated that I was attracted to the same sex. I mean, some of my childhood crushes were on friends who happened to be female. But wasn't that normal?

"It's hot in here," Kiara said, out of the blue.

"It sure is."

"And stank, too."

I laughed. "Some people must've forgot how to use deodorant."

"Or it's just so damn hot in here that deodorant is having a hard time working."

We both sniffed underneath our arms simultaneously.

"Damn," we said at the same time.

"Let's get out of here before we start to contribute to the stank," Kiara said

We headed out the door laughing despite the weight of our conversation still lingering in the air.

chapter eight

Black Bird
————————

The night before my chemistry midterm, my body decided to pull a three-sixty on me. In less than twenty-four hours, my stomach, head and throat went from excellent condition to damn-near total shut-down. I'd already missed two days of school and judging by the fact that I couldn't hold liquids down, it looked like I was about to miss a third. Luckily, my instructor was warm-hearted enough to let me take my exam when I felt better. Whenever that would be.

It was eight-in-the-morning and I was laying in bed shivering with two flannel blankets pulled up to my chin. My stomach was growling but I couldn't even hold down herbal tea. I decided to hold off on my usual breakfast choice of soymilk, toaster waffles and a banana. Instead, I was thinking more along the lines of a plain scrambled egg and maybe a glass of apple juice. I had to put something in my frail body but couldn't get out of bed. So in my best sick voice, I called for reinforcements.

"Mother. Mother." Even though it was early, I knew she'd faithfully be up and ready for work.

She appeared at my door on the verge of panic.

"What's wrong?"

"Nothing," I said, smiling. "You look nice."

She was dressed to the nines in a sharp, white three piece pantsuit. The pants were tailor-made and the jacket hung sleekly to her knees, tapering graciously around her thirty-four inch waist.

She smiled. "Thanks, Babe. How you feeling, this morning?"

"Better, so far. But I only been up a minute."

She felt my forehead. "You still feel kinda warm."

I chuckled because an ice cube would feel warm if it were underneath as many layers as I was.

"You're not going to school today, are you?"
"No. I can't."
"Tell *me* something. You need anything?"
"Actually, I'm kinda hungry."
"Good. After the amount you been throwing up, you need all the food you can get in that little body."
I rolled my eyes, playfully. "I'm not that skinny."
"I know, I know. What do you wanna try to eat?"
"Thought I'd try a scrambled egg."
"Okay. I'll run to the store and get some more orange juice. I got a minute of time to kill before work."

I got out of bed once Mother left the room and peeked out the window. It was raining. It made me smile when I saw the drops hit the window. Back when I was a child, on rainy days, I used to think the entire house was crying. I used to sing and do everything in my power to cheer the house up. Then, when the rain would stop and the sun or a rainbow would make it's grand entrance, I would pretend that it was the house's way of giving me thanks. Isn't is funny how creative we are as children? I wonder at what point, as adults, do we lose our creativity? I wonder why when most adults look outside and see something as amazing as raindrops, they don't see more than just acidic water ruining their paint job?

After breakfast, I decided to catch a glimpse of daytime television. You know, court shows, soap operas, court shows and more soap operas? Since I wasn't in the mood for Divorce Court, I switched the channel to BET; for those of you who aren't into culture, BET stands for Black Entertainment Television. Anyway, I was all curled up on my parent's black, leather couch when the phone rang. I picked up the cordless phone and hit the talk button.

"Hello," I answered in a scratchy, I-feel-sick-as-hell voice.
"Hey, Baby Girl. How you feelin', this morning?"
"Morning? Darius, it's almost noon. It was nice of you to take the time out of your busy schedule and call me."
"I'm sorry. I had a test, this morning."
"In what?" I coughed.
"History."

"How'd you do?"

"Cool, I think. But those true/false questions kicked my ass."

"I heard that."

"You need anything?"

"Not really. Mother cooked me an egg about an hour ago."

"You keepin' it down okay?"

"Yeah." I sat up. "I'm bored, though."

"Yeah? Want me to come keep you company?"

"That'd be nice. Where you at?"

"Up the street, at my homeboy, Carlos' house."

I laughed. Darius had so many homeboys you'd think he were part of a gang.

"What's so funny?"

"Nothing. Just hurry up and get your ass over here."

"You know I love it when you get all demanding, Baby. It make me just want to-"

"Darius, come on." I stopped him. Lately, sex seemed to be the only thing on his mind. It's almost like the more I resisted, the more persistent he became. Well, he could persist all he wanted but just like En Vogue sang a few years back, "He ain't never gonna get it."

"Okay, okay. Just sit pretty. I'll be there in a flash."

"Can't wait." I pressed the 'talk' button, again. Damn. What type of person was I becoming? How long could I hold on to a one-sided relationship just to satisfy my own fears of loneliness? I was becoming heartless. I went into the kitchen to make myself some hot tea. The linoleum felt like ice on my bare feet. After popping a mug of hot water into the microwave, I went into my room to grab my fuzzy slippers. The phone rang before I could even slide my feet in. I knew who it was before I even answered.

"Darius?"

"How'd you know it was me, Babe?"

"I know you by now," I said with a hint of irritation creeping into my voice. "What's up?"

"I called to see if you wanted me to stop and get a movie?"

"We haven't seen *Cooley High* in awhile."

"Baby, we saw it last week."

I laughed. *Cooley High* is the best black film ever made. Back in the day, Kiara and I use to watch it so much, we could recite almost every line. "What about *Friday*?"

"That works. Chris Tucker is funny as hell."

"Ain't that the truth."

"I'll stop by the video store, then be at your house in fifteen minutes. Give or take a minute or two."

"Cool."

"Fifteen then?"

"Fifteen." I hung up the phone. Before I could walk back into the living room, the phone rang, again. Damn that Darius.

"Hello?" I answered the phone feeling irritated. I mean, how many times could one person call?

"Kendall?" It was a female voice.

"Who's this?"

"It's Connie."

"Connie?"

"Keisha's friend, sort of. From the party a few weeks ago?"

I cheesed. "Of course I know who you are." *How could I forget?* "I was just surprised."

"I hope you don't mind me calling. Tomeeka gave me your number."

"I don't mind at all. I'm happy, in fact. I been held captive by this cold for an eternity, it seems." I smoothed down my scattered hair.

"I hate colds. Do you need anything?"

I hesitated. "No, but thank you for asking." I wondered why she was calling me. I mean, I barely knew her. Not that getting to know her was such a bad idea.

"You feeling any better?"

"Much better, actually. It's just a bitch trying to hold food down."

"I know exactly what you mean. I hate colds. Wait, did I already say that?"

I laughed. Our conversation felt mechanical. So, I said:

"How's Tomeeka and Keisha doing? I haven't seen those fools for a few days."

"They're okay. Still arguing."

"As usual," I said.

Then Connie asked:

"What's your major?"

"Pre veterinary medicine."

"Interesting. What made you want to become a veterinarian?"

"I've always dug science." I sat down on the couch. "I used to love animals when I was younger, so veterinary medicine seemed like the way to go."

"Seemed like the way to go? Used to love animals? It doesn't sound like you're very happy with your decision."

"Well, a year ago, I worked for an emergency animal hospital. But I quit and took a job at the place I'm working now. The animal diagnostics lab."

"Wow. A lab technician. That's a reputable job for a twenty-two year old."

"I'm nineteen."

"I thought you looked young. I just didn't want to make you feel bad." She laughed. "Or make myself feel so old."

"How old are you?"

"Twenty-five." She sighed. "Give or take a year or two."

I laughed. "Enough about me. What about you? What brings you to Dryton State Penitentiary?"

She laughed. "I'm an English Major. I'm applying to the Master's program next semester."

"No shit? This is your last undergrad semester?" I coughed then laid down on the couch.

"Yes, it's my fifth year." She laughed, again. "Just your average American college student."

We cracked up.

"So, you wanna be a teacher?"

"Maybe. But I'm more interested in book publishing. I feel that African-American novelists aren't getting the respect they deserve."

"You should talk to my mom. That's the main reason why she started the book store."

"Keisha told me about that. She owns, *A Place Away From Home*, right?"

"That's my Mother."

"I love that place." She paused. "Why'd you quit the emergency hospital? I would think animal interaction would be better than just dealing with specimens all day long. No offense."

"None taken. You're right. I do miss the animals. Treating them. Making them feel pain-free."

"But?"

"But, I hate the politics. Try having to euthanize a viable puppy just because somebody doesn't have the patience to take care of it. It's frustrating."

"Why wouldn't they just give the puppy away to somebody who *can* take care of it?"

"Because a pet is considered property, by law. Regardless of the fact that animals can feel and love."

"That's awful. I can understand your frustration."

We both sat in brief silence.

"Kendall, it sure is refreshing talking to you."

"Thank you. Same to you." I blushed.

"No, I'm serious. My family's from middle America. Colorado to be exact. I moved here five years ago and it's hard finding someone you can relate to."

"What about Keisha?"

She laughed. "I don't really hang out with Keisha. In fact, besides class, the party was the first time we'd even talked." She laughed, again. "She seems cool, though."

"Ghetto Fabulous."

We cracked up.

"So, we should do this, again."

"What?" she asked.

"Talk. It was nice." My heart started to race. Maybe I was sicker than I thought. "I have your number on my caller I.D. Can I call you later?"

"How about now?"

"I'd love to stay on the phone. But unfortunately, I have company coming over."

"I understand. I'll look forward to talking, later."

"Me, too." I was so nervous that I almost didn't hear the doorbell. I stood up from the couch to answer the door. "Maybe we could do lunch." I let Darius in and hugged him softly.

"Hey, Baby Girl." He kissed me on the cheek.
"Well, I don't want to keep you," Connie said.
"Call you later?" I asked.
"I'll look forward to it."

I pushed the 'talk' button. "What took you so long?" I pretended to pout even though, at that point, I didn't give a damn whether he came or not.

"Aw, Baby. I came as soon as I could. The line at the video store was like a mile long. And they didn't even have *Friday*." He wrapped his long arms around my waist.

"So what'd you get?" I reached into the bag that he was holding in his right hand. "*Booty Call*? You have got to be kidding me."

"We never even saw this together."

"Isn't once enough times to see *Booty Call* in one lifetime?" I suddenly understood why Stella was so pissed off at Winston.

He pulled me closer. "Look. I bought some popcorn, too. Kettle corn. It's in the bag."

I looked further into the bag and frowned. How the hell was I supposed to eat greasy-ass popcorn when I could barely hold down chicken broth and eggs?

"Oh, right. You can't eat that, can you?" He looked down at his feet. "I guess I wasn't thinking. Sorry, Baby."

"It's okay. Let's just kick back and watch this damn movie. I'm gonna finish making my tea."

"I'll make it. Carla wouldn't mind if I blew up her kitchen, would she?"

I laughed. Darius couldn't cook for shit. But who was I to criticize? I burn water.

"Hey, Baby?" Darius called out from the kitchen. I could hear him opening and closing cabinets trying to look for the tea. Wouldn't it be easier to just ask?

"Yeah?" I walked into the kitchen and pointed to the canister that contained tea bags.

"Who was you talkin' to when I got here?" He grabbed a mint tea bag.

"Huh?"

"When I got here," he repeated.

"My friend, Connie." I frowned.

"Oh." He placed the tea bag in my cold mug of water.

"Why?" I placed it in the microwave.

"No reason. Just wondering."

"Just wondering? There has to be a reason for wondering."

"Well, it just seems like lately, every time I come over, you on the phone."

"Every time you come over? This was the first time. What're you talking about?"

"Okay, so this was the first time. But why you get off so quick?"

"As opposed to talking on the phone while you're here? Isn't that considered rude?"

He blushed. "Guess I'm overreacting, huh?"

"Let's just watch this damn movie." I smiled.

"Sounds cool. You want some soup?"

"Not right now." I was starting to feel nauseated.

"Well, you mind if I heat up this popcorn?"

* * *

"What they doin'?"

My fist playfully made contact with Darius' shoulder for the damn-near hundredth time. *Booty Call* had been on for less than an hour and there were already too many sex scenes and sexual innuendoes to count on two hands. And every time one of the lame-ass characters initiated or engaged in the act of 'movie sex', Darius pointed to the screen in a desperate attempt to spark up a sexual conversation.

"Ouch." He playfully rubbed his shoulder.

"Then stop asking dumb questions." I leaned back with my head resting on his chest. He smelled like deodorant and popcorn.

He wrapped his long arms across my chest.

I adjusted my position to make sure his arms didn't 'accidentally' brush up against my breasts. Again.

"This movie is the shit and you know it."

"You mean, this movie *is* shit."

"You know you like this movie, Girl." He squeezed me tighter and kissed my neck.

I continued to watch the movie.

He continued to kiss my neck. Then he turned my face to the side with his right hand and gently kissed my lips.

"How am I gonna get to see the movie if you keep messing with me?"

"Okay, okay. But you know how I get when we're alone, Baby." I squirmed. "Yeah, but you're the one who rented it."

"But how you know I rented it to watch it?" He reached over and gently squeezed my left breast.

"I'm sick, remember?" I slid away from him in disgust.

"Well, ain't that a shock. It's always something."

I sat up and faced him. "What the hell is that supposed to mean? I'm sick. How is that an excuse?"

"Today, you're sick. Just like the last time you had to get to class. And the time before that, you had to pick up your moms from work even though I know she has her own damn car."

"You're overreacting. Why should I make excuses? And what for?"

"You know damn well what for, Kendall. I'm talking about affection. Do I have the plague?" He sniffed his underarms. "Do I stank?"

"That's ridiculous. I always show you affection."

He crossed his arms over his chest like a five-year-old who was just told he couldn't have anymore cookies until after dinner.

"What is this really about? Sex? 'Cause you know how I feel about that. You knew when we first got together. I don't wanna rush into it. I want it to be special. I want it to be magical."

His face softened and he locked his hands into mine. "But it will be special, Baby. Just trust me and let me be your first. I'm begging." He leaned forward and covered my lips with his.

Didn't he hear one word I said? Probably not since his manhood was already protruding. I pushed him away, once again.

"Come on, baby." He leaned me back on the couch and pinned my body down with his own.

I tried to protest but his lips were forcibly pressed against mine. His body was pressed so tight against me, I could hardly breathe. I struggled to get up and eventually slid from underneath him.

"Didn't you hear me? I said no and I meant it. If you can't respect that then get the hell out." I was standing at that point.

"Oh, so now you throwing me out? Just because I wanna make out with my girl? Is that a damn crime?" He stood up, facing me.

"It's a violation as far as I'm concerned. It's my body and if I don't wanna be touched, I shouldn't be touched. Respect my decision."

"A violation? To kiss my own girlfriend?"

"Lower your voice in my parent's house. Have some respect."

"I'll lower my voice. But first hear this."

"I'm listening."

"I'm a man. I have needs. How much longer are you gonna make me wait?"

"As long as I say. Making love is a two way street otherwise it's just one person getting screwed. I'm not down with that. You should be man enough to accept that."

"You need to start thinking about someone other than yourself sometimes."

"Think about somebody other than myself? Fuck that, Darius. This is the one thing I'm allowed to be selfish about. It's my body and nobody else's. You're the selfish one. You need to learn to think with the right head. Then maybe I would've considered sharing my body with you. That idea's over, now."

"Over? You mean you're never gonna-"

"Never was."

"I wasted over a year for something you never had any intentions of giving me, anyway?"

His words hit my body like a swarm of killer bees. "I can't deal with this shit. If you don't love me enough to wait, then you don't deserve me."

"I don't deserve you? What the hell kind of conceited-ass statement is that? What do you think this is? You expect me to wait forever? Just treat you right, do everything to make you happy and get nothing in return. Wake up, Kendall. We ain't in high school no more. We're adults, this is the real world not a fairy tale."

"The real world? So in order for me to be treated the way I should be treated I have to do something against my will? Just let you have a sacred part of me for a lousy dinner or a few bunches of roses?" I could feel the heat rising rapidly around my neck creating a thick film of sweat.

Darius lowered his head.

"What are you trying to prove? You think this ring is supposed to mean you own me or something? Well, I don't belong to any being on this earth. And I'm not doing anything against my will." I spoke calmly. Kind of like a calm wild. You know the point when your mind feels so much rage that your body can't physically keep up so you have no choice but to relax and talk calmly before you explode? Or better yet, before you implode.

"A thousand dollars says I own something."

"It's good to know I meant that much to you. At least I found out how much of an asshole you are *before* I fell in love."

I could see the hot air flowing from his ears.

"That's okay. You can have this back." I placed the ring in his palm. "It turned my finger green, anyway. You worthless asshole. That's why I been seeing James. You naive, son-of-a-bitch." Once the words rolled off my lips, I almost wanted to take them back.

He stared at me for a moment as if he was just shot in the chest with a forty-five.

My lips started to tremble in fear. I was afraid of how badly I hurt him. Afraid of what he might do next.

I never saw it coming. Everything moved in slow motion and I could see the vengeful energy building up from his chest, to his neck and finally releasing through his open right hand to the left side of my face.

I didn't cry. In fact, I didn't say a word. The built-up rage inside of me erased the physical pain, momentarily. I touched the left side of my cheek with my right hand, then balled up the same hand in a mighty fist. I returned Darius' favor with a right cross to his left jaw.

"Shit, Kendall." He held his jaw. "I think you broke my fuckin' jaw."

That's when the tears started to fall. Not the tears of a weak victim but the tears of an enraged, violated woman. A woman who deserved to be treated like the princess her father always told her she was. My father, Mr. Thomas Reed, would never hit a woman.

"I'm so sorry, Kendall." He had the nerve to reach out and stroke the same cheek that moments earlier he struck. "I promise I won't do it again. I-I just got carried away."

That's when I really lost it:

"Don't touch me, Darius. You're damn right you won't do it, again. Or anything to me, again. Ever."

"What's that supposed to mean?"

"It means, it's over. You and me. Us. I can't take this shit anymore. Just get the hell out. I don't wanna see your face, anymore. Please go."

He opened his mouth to speak.

"Go," I spoke before he could. "Now." I turned my back and headed to my room without looking back. I didn't wait for the door to close nor did I wait for him to say goodbye. I was finally rid of Darius' trifling ass for good. I was free: like a black bird with broken wings.

chapter nine

Fishing and Conversation

Dear Reader,

It's days like this when I miss him most. Days when dark clouds shield the beauty of the pale-blue sky and capture the sun. Days when the air reeks of wet cedar wood and the leaves of grass are moving rhythm-less. It was on days like this when my father and I used to go fishing.

"Wanna go catch some fish?"

That's all my ten-year-old ears needed to hear. I'd jump out of bed energetically at eight-in-the-morning, heart racing with a permanent grin on my face. "Tom and Jerry," "Alvin and the Chipmunks" and even my favorite Bugs Bunny special was mentally replaced by visions of casting my line into the water and reeling in all the fish in the world. After all, in my mind, my father was the greatest fisherman ever.

My fondest memory of fishing was the preliminary ritual of going to the bait store. I'll never forget the nauseating smell of rotten fish and dried earthworms pounding my nostrils. I remember running through the store like a fat rat in a cheese factory, grabbing every edible item my tiny, yellow hands could carry. Big Hunks, Nerds, strawberry soda and those little chocolate cakes covered in marshmallow and coconut were my favorite fishing snacks. While my father was at the counter purchasing various Styrofoam containers full of earthworms and minnows, I was running through the store taking a mental inventory of all the goods I could con him into buying me.

"You gonna eat all that?" my father would bellow every time I joined him at the counter with my final selection of snacks: a task that usually required more than one trip.

I'd always laugh while dumping my junk on the counter next to my father's own junk-selection: a six pack of beer, barbecue potato chips, liverwurst, honey ham, cheddar cheese singles and a loaf of bread. At nine-in-the-morning, sandwiches and junk food would be the heart of our breakfast. It was a momentary break from my normal breakfast routine of Fruity Pebbles or instant apple cinnamon-flavored oatmeal.

What I loved best about fishing was the smell of the outdoors. I loved the way the muddy, salty lake lightly caressed my sensory organs. I loved the smell of the rich, turbid earth mixed with the piney scent of the rustling, spring leaves. The rich smell of the peaceful outdoors created a smooth, intoxicating tranquility that was much needed in my juvenile life. Everything, including Gods' smallest creatures, seemed to respect the calm, serene moment in nature.

Conversation between my father and I usually consisted of me running my mouth constantly about anything and everything that came to mind. My father was not a talkative person, but when he did speak, my ears were blessed with a valuable story.

"My Grandpa Rick use to take me fishing when I was your age."

"You were my age, before?"

"Of course, Little Bit. I was a kid, just like you."

"Did you catch a lot of fish?"

"We caught enough fish to feed a village. But there was one time when we didn't catch anything all day."

"Kind of like, today."

"Yes." My father laughed. "Kind of like today. Except, right when we were about to give up, Grandpa's pole was almost pulled in the water. He grabbed his pole in the nick of time and started to pull. The sucker was so big it almost pulled him right off the bank, into the water."

"What'd you do?"

"Let me finish my story, Little Bit. I grabbed on to Grandpa's waist and started pulling. I could've sworn we had caught a whale. But we didn't. After about an hour, Grandpa had worn the fish out and pulled it to the bank. I grabbed the net but the fish was too big for the net."

"What'd you do, Daddy?" I started to become antsy.

Fishing and Conversation

"We did nothing. Grandpa cut the line. I was mad at him for it, too. But then he said something to me, I'll never forget. He said 'Boy, always show respect to anything that gives up that much fight.' And I always will."

When conversation started to get too deep, I would always break the solemn shift with a joke or two.

"Knock, knock."

"Who's there?"

"Joe."

"Joe who?"

"Joe Mama."

Daddy always laughed hysterically at my lame jokes regardless of the amount of times I enlightened him with my creativity. And it always made me feel good to hear him laugh so I'd usually keep going until he gave me an indirect sign to let me know he was becoming bored or agitated. One of the easiest signs was for him to ask me to pass him the liverwurst. We were so close.

"They just not bitin' today, huh, Little Bit?"

The moment my father said those words, I always knew it was time to reel in my bait and start packing up the breakfast residue. There were never any fish to string up, as far as I can remember.

The car ride home was always silent. I guess I could blame it on fatigue. But I'd like to think our silence was a way to soak in the pleasant contents of our moments. For me, fishing was a way to escape the hustle of the real world. It was a way to escape the norm of spelling tests and peanut butter and jelly sandwiches. Fishing was a way to escape life for just a few hours and pretend that there were no worries or sadness. And at that moment in time, nothing else existed except for me and my father.

These are the days I miss him most.

chapter ten

Drowning Your Sorrows in Friendship and Wine

"So, just like that, he hit you?"

"Yeah, Girl. Just like that."

The night after the breakup, I was sitting up at the Seafood Shack with Connie. I thought about calling Tomeeka but didn't feel like hearing , "I told you so" or "Just give him one more chance." Know what I mean? So that's how I ended up eating warm crab legs dipped in hot garlic butter with a girl I knew very little about.

"Are you okay? Are you hurt?"

"No, I'm not hurt." I touched my left cheek. It was slightly swollen. "Not physically anyway."

"What a bastard. Who does he think he is, hitting on a woman like that?" She put down the crab leg she was working on and sat back in her chair.

"Yeah, I know. It pisses me off every time I think about it. What an asshole. I never even guessed he was the type. You know?"

"Yeah, but most people never know until it happens. It's hard to judge people like that."

"That's for damn sure." I dipped a piece of crabmeat into the seasoned butter. "But you think I would've known after a year."

"A year? That's a long time. He's never shown any signs of violence before?"

"Never. I mean, he's yelled a few times. But I've yelled at him even more. Know what I mean?"

She nodded her head and leaned forward, resting both hands on the table.

"Well, there was the time at the party. But he only grabbed me." I started to feel like a fool. The signs were there all along.

"I remember. I just didn't think it was an appropriate thing to mention."

"I guess I should've put a stop to it right then and there."

"But it's hard with love. Love can turn the most grounded person into a fool."

"Ain't that the truth. But with Darius, it wasn't even about love."

"Then what was it about?" She took a sip of her white wine.

"Convenience, I guess. But that's kind of a stupid reason, don't you think?" I took a sip of my raspberry iced-tea.

"No, it's not stupidity. It's reality."

"Yeah, it's called marriage." I laughed.

Connie chuckled.

"Look at me. I invited you out on a Saturday night and here I am dumping all my problems on you. I'm sorry."

"Hey, don't be sorry. I'm just happy I can be here for you. I know I don't help much with advice but feel free to dump whatever you want on me." She smiled.

I smiled back. I could feel myself blushing.

"Can you excuse me for a minute?"

I watched as she strolled away towards the bathroom. She looked cute in her dark blue, tight fitted jeans and dark brown hippy-type shirt. Her feet were barely covered in leather, single-strapped sandals. I felt underdressed in my black, carpenter-style jeans, white polo shirt and white shell-toed shoes. Tomeeka and Keisha would have a fit if they knew I confided in Connie, first. But I wanted a non-biased, educated opinion. You know? I needed someone who knew me as a woman hurting and Darius as the dog who did it. Know what I mean?

"Penny for your thoughts?" Connie's return startled me, at first.

"I was just thinking about how stuffed I am," I said, motioning around the table at the crab exoskeletons piled on random plates.

She took her seat. "So, you're finally finished eating?"

"Finally?"

"You sure can pack it down."

I laughed. "Hey, you didn't do so bad your damn self."

"I guess I didn't exactly eat light. But how can you, when something tastes so good?"

"Ain't that the truth." I looked around for the waiter.

"So, what else do you do with your time besides write?"

"Well, I have two jobs."

I leaned in closer.

"The first one is at The Bank of Dryton."

"As a teller?"

"Yes, after school, four days a week. And the other one is on Saturday's only. I tutor some of the kids that society has labeled as 'underprivileged'."

I nodded my head, slowly. Connie was becoming more and more amazing to me, by the second. "How'd you get into that?"

"What? Tutoring?"

"Yeah." I finally found the waiter and motioned for him to come to our table.

"Well, my freshman composition instructor recommended me. She's the founder of the program, Aim High."

"Aim High? What's that?"

"How was everything, Ladies?" The waiter appeared at our table and began to bus our empty plates.

"It was delicious but we're ready for our check-"

"Can I interest you two in one of our decadent deserts? Our pecan pie is said to be the best in Dryton." The waiter interrupted me with a bright smile.

"I'm stuffed." Connie rubbed her belly.

"Me, too. We'll actually just take our check." There was a slight hesitation in my voice. I mean, he said it was the best pecan pie in Dryton.

"A light, delicious brown sugar filling with roasted pecans, topped with our chef's special blend of cinnamon-sugar and caramel. And to top it all off we have homemade vanilla bean ice-cream just like mom's." The waiter gave me a toothy grin.

Ten minutes later, I was digging into warm pie and rich, vanilla bean ice-cream.

Connie sipped on a hot, hazelnut latte'. "Anyway, Aim High, is an organization aimed to keep school kids off the streets. What we basically do is try to make our program more desirable than hanging out on the corners, selling drugs and going to Juvenile Hall."

I nodded with a mouthful of pie. My Grandma's pie could kick this pie's ass. The pecans weren't even fresh.

"We do things like take the kids hiking, to amusement parks and help those who are having trouble in school."

"What age groups are involved?"

"Mostly first through sixth grade. But we do have a nice handful of teenagers who come regularly. There are at least thirty active members of Aim High. And we've only been active for a few years."

I paused for a moment, pushing back my empty plate. "That's amazing. I really admire you."

She blushed.

"I'll be your cashier when you're ready." The waiter slid the check on the edge of the table.

We both reached for it at the same time.

"I'll get it," Connie offered.

"No, I'm the one who invited you. Let me get it."

"But I wanted to come and I'm having a good time."

"But I have the check," I said with the check in my hand.

Connie smiled awkwardly as I reached into my purse for my ATM card.

"I'm having a good time, too." I handed my card to the eager waiter.

"Hey, the night's still young." She leaned forward and smiled. "You still haven't told me much about yourself. Why don't we go to my place."

"Sounds like a plan to me."

"But I'm concerned about one thing."

"What's that?"

"Are you going to be okay?"

"You mean after what happened with Darius?"

"No, I mean after all the food you ate. That's more than I've ever seen one person consume in one sitting."

I laughed loudly causing an older couple to look my way and smile.

Drowning Your Sorrows in Friendship and Wine

* * *

"So how old were you when your father left?"

"About ten. I was devastated, let me tell you."

We were sitting on Connie's beige couch, sipping on wine coolers and munching on honey-wheat pretzels. I had my shoes off since I felt so comfortable in the cozy, one-bedroom apartment. When I first entered the apartment, I have to admit, I was impressed; the soft earth tones and dark woods, reminded me of the decor of a young businesswoman rather than that of a college student.

"And you said you have one older brother? That's your only sibling?"

"Yes. His name is Todd. He's in the navy and will be twenty-eight in June."

"So, he's only three years older?"

"Yes, give or take a month or two. I'm a February baby."

"A Valentines Day gift," I said with an involuntary sigh.

"What's wrong?"

"Nothing really. I was just thinking about being alone on V-Day."

"Come on, Kendall. I'm sure there'll be guys lined up waiting to take you out." She sucked on a pretzel stick.

I smiled.

"I understand how you feel, though. Me and my ex broke up one week before Valentine's Day, last year."

"Your ex? Was it a long-term relationship?" I took a sip of my melon-flavored wine cooler.

"Five years. So, yeah, I guess you can say long-term." She laid her head back on the couch.

"Damn. Five years. I thought one-year was long."

She smiled, taking a sip of her berry-flavored wine cooler.

"So, what happened?"

"I guess we just kind of grew apart. There was really no fault. It just started to feel more like a business relationship than a romantic one. Somewhere in between rent and groceries, all the fire was gone."

"That's sad. That's the way it was with me and Darius after only one month. For me, anyway."

Connie nodded. "Were you and Darius ever friends?"

I thought for a moment. "I guess you can say that's all we ever were. Just friends. I never felt anything for him, romantically." I felt my words start to slur. I placed my drink down on the table. Slurring was definitely my limit. I mean, I couldn't start talking about shit I'd regret in the morning. Know what I mean?

"It's funny how many people stay together even after the romance is gone." Connie was starting to slur, as well.

"Yeah, it's almost like an obligation rather than a choice."

"Exactly. People become so afraid of being alone they forget about making themselves happy. And suddenly they wake up and find that their independence is lost."

We both sat in silence, consumed within our own thoughts in a melancholy state of physical and emotional drunkenness.

"So back to your previous relationship." I was the first to break the silence.

"Huh?" Connie jumped at the sudden interruption.

"Your ex? Did he go to Dry U? I mean, do I know him?"

"No. *He* definitely does not go to Dry U." She paused. "Can I get you another drink?"

"No, two is my limit. I have to drive home and I'm feeling buzzed already. Besides, I'm underage, remember?"

"Well, underage or not, if you're feeling as buzzed as I feel, you probably shouldn't drive."

"Maybe I'll just stay here a little while longer." I stood up to throw my empty bottle away. My head started to spin as I resumed forward.

"So, do you think you'll pursue that James guy?" Connie called out.

"I don't think so." I sat back down on the couch. "Not after such a violent breakup with Darius."

"Yeah, that's a smart thing to do."

"What about you? Are you dating anyone, right now?"

"Not at the moment. With work and school on my shoulders, where do I find the time?"

"I feel you."

"And to be quite frank with you, I haven't found anybody I'm interested in. Well, maybe one person but-" Her voice trailed off.

"But what?" I glanced over and fell into her beckoning, brown eyes. Or maybe it was the alcohol cussing me out.

"What was I saying?" Connie asked, still in my eyes.

I looked down at the carpet and blushed.

"Whoa."

"Shit starts to creep up on you, huh?" I said, finally finding my voice.

"No kidding. I think it's time to call it quits."

We both stood up at the same time and walked towards the front door.

"You sure you're okay to drive?"

"Yeah, I'm okay." I smoothed down my jeans. It's nothing like a few moments of awkwardness to sober you up. Know what I mean? Besides, I had to get home. I mean, what kind of person would she think I was if I crashed on her couch after only two drinks?

"You don't look okay. Maybe you should stay. I wouldn't mind." Her eyes found mine again.

"I don't even feel buzzed, anymore. I promise, I'm okay." I damn-near ran out the front door.

Deep down inside, I knew I would never be okay.

chapter eleven

Dreams in a Bottle

On Friday, somewhere in the middle of March, I decided to go home early from school. I really don't know why I did it. It wasn't like I was sick or anything. I just didn't feel like being bothered by anybody. I was tired of chemistry, sick of English and damn-near ready to burn my calculus book.

Not to mention the fact that I was ovulating and the referred pain on the left side of my groin was kicking my caramel-colored ass.

I arrived home at around noontime and was surprised to see Daddy's white, Cadillac Seville parked in the driveway.

"Hey, Daddy. What you doin' home? Everything okay?" I bombarded him with questions before my backpack even left my shoulders.

"Yeah, everything's fine. It was slow so I took a personal day." He stood up and kissed me on the cheek. "No reason why the other mechanics can't run the shop every once in awhile."

"I heard that," I said with a sigh of relief. "Guess it pays to be the boss."

"You better believe it. What you doing home from school so early? I thought this was your late day."

"I needed a break." I smiled. It was good to know that he actually paid attention to my life.

"I heard that. We all need a break sometimes. The daily grind starts to kick you down after awhile." He sat back down in his favorite recliner. "You wanna watch something?"

"No, I think I'll lay down for awhile." I headed towards my room.

"You feelin' okay?"

I stopped and turned around to face him. I noticed that he didn't have a beer in his hand. "I feel fine. Just tired is all."

"Well, you know you can talk to me whenever you feel like talking."

I managed a weak smile. I started thinking back to how easy it used to be to talk to Daddy. Things were so much easier, then. I remember going to Daddy when Craig, my third grade enemy, kept hitting me in class. It's kind of ironic that I didn't go to him with the Darius incident. I wonder what Daddy's response would be now? I'll bet it would be a little different than, "That just means he likes you, Kendall."

"You hungry? I can go get something from the store to cook. Or we can go out."

"Sounds nice but maybe later. I think I'll just take a nap, for now."

"Well, why don't you lay down on the couch."

"I wanna lay in my own bed." I went inside my room and closed the door before he could respond. I just needed to sleep. I thought about those little blue pills that Mother used to take whenever she needed "rest". I wondered if she had any left. I went into the bathroom to search the medicine cabinet. There was aspirin, ibuprofen and antacids but no blue pills. I went into my parents room to see if I could find them there. Sure enough there they were; the bottle of 'sleep aid' was sitting on the nightstand next to Mother's side of the bed. I took two pills out of the bottle and headed back to my room. Both pills slid down my throat easily with a small sip of water. I started thinking:

Why was a nineteen-year-old grown woman still living with mommy and daddy? Was I scared? Scared of being alone? Is that why I stayed with Darius so long? Yes, I pay for my own car, clothes and school. But Connie pays for the same shit, plus she has her own apartment.

I smiled at the thought of Connie. And within minutes, I was sound asleep.

* * *

"Kendy. Kendy. Come eat."

I slowly opened my eyes. I noticed that my room was dark even though my blinds were open. Did night already creep in?

"Hey, Kendy. Wake up. You have to eat *something*." I recognized the voice as Mother's even though I could only see her silhouette.

"Huh?"

"You feeling okay? Your Daddy said you been sleep since noon. You not getting sick, again, are you?"

"I'm not sick. I'm fine." I sat up with my eyes still halfway closed. "What time is it?"

"Almost nine. I would've let you sleep but you know how I am about you eating."

"Yeah, I guess I should eat." I sat up and clicked on my lamp. I smacked my lips together. My mouth felt like the Mohave Desert.

"You guess so? Where my belt?"

"Okay, Mother. I'm getting up."

"Tell *me* something."

I laughed. "What'd you cook?"

"Baked chicken, garlic pasta and zucchini with mushrooms."

"Tore the kitchen up, huh?"

"You know it." She started to close the door. "Kendy?"

"Yeah?"

"You'd tell me if something was wrong, huh?"

"Of course, I would." I felt bad about lying but how could I tell her what was wrong when I didn't really know what was wrong myself?

She smiled then left the room.

I stood up and stretched my legs. My limbs felt like jelly and my head felt like a small hammer was rhythmically pounding against the back of my skull. I felt like crap. What the hell was wrong with me? Mentally, I just wasn't feeling right. Almost as if I no longer knew the reason for my existence. Maybe my feelings were due to the fact that at nineteen-years-old, I couldn't keep a stable relationship. Or maybe because, at nineteen-years-old, I didn't know what I wanted to do when I 'grew up'. Whatever that means.

The phone rang. The sudden sharpness of the ring made my heart beat fast.

"Hello." I picked up on the first ring.

"Hey, Kendy. What's up?"

"Tomeeka?"

"Yup, it's me. You was sleep?"

"No, I was just about to eat, actually. What's up?"

"Not much. Just goin' to school, throwin' up and sleepin' all damn day."

"Glad it ain't me, Girl."

"Who you tellin'? I'm retainin' enough water to fill Lake Dryton."

"When's the baby due?"

"Mid-August."

"That soon? You ready?"

"Got no choice but to be ready. You know?"

I nodded even though she couldn't see through the phone. "When you telling Marcus? You're starting to show."

"Yeah, I know. Luckily, I haven't been givin' him none, lately. And I been tryin' to wear baggier shirts and stuff."

After a short period of silence, Tomeeka finally spoke up. "Kendy, I know you been down, lately. And I don't wanna make you feel worse."

"But?"

"But there's somethin' I need to talk to you about. Somethin' that's been on my mind for awhile now."

I sat in silence waiting. I hate when people beat around the bush.

"It's somethin' that's been botherin' me and I need to get it out before I explode."

"What is it?"

"Well, I can't say names yet. 'Cause the people I'm talkin' about will get theirs soon enough."

"Okay. So no names. Just tell me what's up."

"Okay. I have proof that somebody is doin' wrong. I have direct proof but I don't know what to do 'cause it's hurtful."

"Tomeeka, what're you trying to say?"

"Well, let's just pretend like you caught your best friend with your man. And you knew about it first hand. Who would you approach? Your best friend or your man?"

I thought long and hard. "Both, I guess. I mean, it all depends on who I cared about the most. And it also depends on the evidence I had. 'Cause I wouldn't wanna make false accusations and ruin both relationships."

"Let's just say that I, I mean you caught them in the act but they didn't know it."

"So let me get this straight."

"Yeah."

"I caught my best friend and boyfriend in bed? But didn't disturb them? What would I do?"

"Uh huh."

"First of all, they never would've gone undisturbed. I would've confronted their naked asses right in the act. But in your scenario, I would kick the dude to the curb, right away. Then, I'd have to cool down before I ended the friendship with my best friend. I'd have to cool down 'cause otherwise I'd probably knock her out. I mean, you can expect that shit from a dude."

"That shit happens everyday on Jerry and Ricki. You can't trust nobody these days."

I sat quietly wondering what she was getting around to. Did she catch Marcus and Keisha together? Thick, nappy-haired Keisha? I laughed out loud.

"What's so funny?" she asked.

"Nothing. I just had a crazy thought."

"Well it ain't funny. This type of shit breaks up friendships all the time."

"Tomeeka cut the bullshit. It's me you're talking to. The one you can trust, remember?"

"Yeah." She let out a weak but audible sigh. "But this is the one time I can't tell you. Soon as the guilty parties are exposed, you'll find out."

"Is it Keisha?"

"Kendy, come on."

"You come on, Meeka. This ain't the kind of shit you just halfway tell somebody."

"I know but I can't talk about it. And you the one I always talk to. Since I met you, I've told you more than I've told anybody in the twenty-years I been on this earth."

"Thanks," I said politely even though I was growing more and more impatient by the second.

"Trust me, okay? I can't tell you specifically. All I can say is I'm hurtin' inside and with the baby comin' and me havin' to tell Marcus, I can't deal with this stress. I just made it through my first trimester."

"Only two more to go." I laughed.

"Thanks for remindin' me." She giggled. "But on the real, you like a sister to me. I had to tell you what's been eatin' me. Even though I know you still bent up over Darius' triflin' ass."

"I'm not bent up over Darius. His ass was dismissed long before he hit me."

"Well, I guess that's as good a reason as any. But who am I to talk? I can't even count the number of times Marcus put me on the ground."

"Once is enough for me." I absently picked at a small bump that was forming on my chin.

"Yeah, I know what you mean. I can't have that shit around my baby girl."

"Baby girl? You know the sex, already?"

She laughed. "Calm down. I just want a girl. I figure if I say it enough, my wish might come true."

"You something else, Meeka. I better get to the kitchen. I'm starvin' like Marvin'."

"You need to eat somethin'. Seems like your ass is gettin' skinnier by the minute."

I frowned, running my hand over my concaved belly. I had lost five pounds in one week. Could people really tell?

"Don't worry. I'm just jokin' with you. You too beautiful to be considered skinny. I'll let you go. Take care of yourself, okay?"

"Okay."

"And make sure you remember that I love you and would never do anything to hurt you."

"Now you trying to get all sentimental on me and crap."

"Forget you, Tramp. I was just sayin'."

"Later, Meeka."

"Later."

I hung up the phone and just sat in my bed for a minute. Was Keisha sleeping with Marcus? How could you sleep with your own roommate's man? And the same man who fathered her child, too. In my eyes, that kind of mess should be punishable by law. But if it were a crime to cheat, the jail would be overrun with infidels. Know what I mean?

chapter twelve

Unexpected Bliss

"How's the letter writing going?"
"Letter? What letter?"
"The one you were going to write your father?"
I shrugged my shoulders. "I don't know."
"Have you started writing it, yet?"
"No."
"Is it too difficult?"
"I never tried. So I don't know."
Dr. Porsche sat back in her chair. Her blue eyes displayed pure frustration, an emotion that seemed to defy the laws of psychotherapy.
I shifted my eyes to the ground. I couldn't help the fact that I felt irritable and withdrawn. What was wrong with acting out my own emotions? I was in a therapy office, wasn't I?
"Kendall, tell me what's on your mind?"
"What do you mean?"
"I think you know what I mean." She raised her left eyebrow at me.
I sat back in my seat, arms crossed, shoulders slumped.
"How are things going with your mom?"
"Mother and I are fine."
"Your sister?"
"She's okay. I haven't talked to her in a minute, though."
"Do you miss her?"
"Always. We both get kind of busy. But she knows I think about her." I paused. "And I know she thinks about me, too."
Dr. Porsche smiled. "How's school going?"
"It's going. The workload is hard this semester. Chemistry is kicking my ass."

"I remember those days all too well." She chuckled. "But you can handle it, right? You need extra help?"

"No, I'm handling it. I've been having trouble sleeping, though. Some nights I have to take sleeping pills. But I got a 'B' on my chemistry midterm. So it all seems to be working out okay."

Dr. Porsche sat back, looking perplexed. She wiped invisible sweat from her forehead.

I decided to speak up. "Lately, I've been feeling down. Really down."

"In what way?"

"I don't really know. It feels like I'm constantly PMS-ing. It takes me an hour to get out of bed and get dressed, these days."

"Did anything in particular happen?"

"Nothing in particular. Everything is getting to me, I guess." I subconsciously touched the side of my face that Darius hit.

"Hmm. Have you talked to your father, lately?"

"Life doesn't revolve around my father. I mean have you talked to *your* father, lately?"

"Kendall, I wasn't insinuating that life revolves around your father. I just wanted to know if you've been spending any more time with him."

"I know what you were insinuating. And it's not always that easy to pinpoint a person's problems. Yes, my father's an alcoholic. But that doesn't mean that every time I feel down, it's related to that."

"Kendall, I wasn't trying to-"

"No, let me finish." I interrupted her. I mean, I was paying her to listen, right?

She sat back in her chair with her arms crossed and an uneasy smile on her face.

"Did you even notice that the big rock on my finger is missing?" I raised my voice an octave.

"Yes, Kendall, I noticed. But it's not my job to bring up things that you've never spoken about."

"But it *is* your job to insinuate that all my problems are centered around my father? Have you wondered why I've never talked about guys in here?"

"Of course I wonder, Kendall."

"Well, let me tell you, Dr. Porsche. I don't like guys. I never have. And I don't think I ever will since I've never been mentally attracted to a guy."

"I'm sorry to hear that. Have you ever thought about why?"

"Why what?"

"Why you're not mentally attracted to guys?"

"You mean like because of my father?" I started to calm down, a little.

"No. In my experiences in life, with clients and in books I've read, I don't think a negative male role model can cause a person not to be attracted to the opposite sex."

"Meaning?"

"Meaning, human beings usually develop their attraction towards the opposite sex or same sex through a combination of learned and genetic traits. Usually when a young girl or boy experiences negativity from a role model, it doesn't terminate their feelings towards that sex altogether. Of course it can affect the way they view that particular sex."

"You mean by making them feel attracted towards a person who doesn't resemble the negative role model?" I uncrossed my arms and sat forward in my seat.

"Sometimes, yes. For example, a friend of mine had an abusive father. So, in turn, she always seemed to fall in love with men who were pushovers."

"I see. So she could make sure she was never abused?"

"Possibly. And I also know similar situations where the woman will pick abusive men because that's all she knows. You understand what I'm saying?"

I nodded my head in understanding. But why didn't I possess *any* feelings for the opposite sex?

"Can I ask you a personal question, off the record?" She put down her writing tablet.

"Go for it."

"When you say, 'mentally attracted', what do you mean?"

"I mean, I've never romantically clicked with a guy. I think some guys are cute. And a few are even sexy, to me. But that's about it. It's always like a far away attraction towards a guy I never met. But when I get to know him, the feelings are suddenly over." I paused. "It's hard to explain."

"So, initially, the attraction is there but when it's time to get close, the attraction vanishes?"

"Exactly. Take this guy James, I met. For a minute, I thought he was sexy. His outer appearance, I mean. But after a few conversations at school, I don't even think he's cute. We don't have anything to talk about, really. It's not like when I talk to Connie."

"Connie?"

"Yeah, I just met her about a month ago. We get along so good. And the past few weeks we've almost developed a friendship stronger than Tomeeka, who I've known for a year."

Dr. Porsche smiled.

I looked at the clock.

"Don't worry about the time. You're my last appointment. Tell me more about Connie."

"Well, she's an English major. And she helps kids in her spare time. She has her own apartment because she works at a bank. Isn't that ambitious?"

Dr. Porsche nodded and smiled.

I continued to talk about Connie for the next half-hour. At that moment, I felt better than I'd felt in days. And when I left Dr. Porsche's office, I felt rejuvenated and refreshed. I felt as if I was ready to take on the world.

Then I touched the left side of my face and suddenly felt the world crawling back on my shoulders.

chapter thirteen

Rule #1:
Expect the Unexpected

On Saturday I was ripped from a wake-less slumber by the sound of the doorbell. I abruptly sat up in bed, heart racing one-thousand times per minute and looked at the clock. Damn. It was two-in-the-afternoon. How the hell did I sleep in so long?

Through the closed door, I could make out muffled voices coming from the living room. I stood up slowly so I wouldn't get a head rush and opened the blinds. The sunlight burned my eyes. It was a beautiful day outside; it was one of those perfect spring days that usually entails barbecue and volleyball at some tree-filled park. But despite the day and it's loveliness, I felt like crap. My body felt like lead and my head felt like I'd been sitting up at some construction site in the middle of downtown San Francisco.

It was time to lay off the pills.

"Kendy." I heard Mother yell from the living room.

"Damn." I slid on my slippers.

"Kendy?" She was getting closer.

I opened the door.

"Kendy?"

"Yeah, Mother?"

"Lazarus has risen." Mother raised both hands in the air. "I thought you was trying to stay in bed all day, again." She lowered her arms and smiled. She was already dressed in white Capri's and a lime green shirt.

"I'm up." I smiled as I walked down the hallway into the living room. "Who was at the door?" I stopped dead in my tracks as I came face-to-face with a familiar smile.

"Good afternoon, sleepy head," Connie said.

"Hey. What you doing here?" I spoke loudly in hopes of averting her attention from my cut-off sweats and thin, cotton tank top. I folded my arms across my chest.

"Well, I haven't talked to you in a few days and was just wondering how you're doing."

"I'm good." I absently fingered a tiny, moth-eaten hole on the right side of my tank top.

"Glad to hear it. I would've called first but my cell phone went out in the car."

I smiled not knowing what else to say. I let my fingers run through my hair which, of course, was flying every which way but the right way.

"Kendy, aren't you gonna invite Connie to sit down or something?" Mother cut in. "She did come all the way over here to see you."

I smiled, embarrassed. "Sorry, Connie. Have a seat. You thirsty or anything?"

"No thanks. I'm fine." She took a seat on the loveseat facing the TV.

I sat down as far away from her as I could. I mean, who wanted to smell morning breath at two-in-the-afternoon?

"Well, Kendy, I'm on my way to Mama's house. You need anything while I'm gone?"

"No, I don't need anything. Thanks, though."

"Uh-huh. It was nice meeting you, Connie."

"It was nice meeting you, too, Mrs. Reed." Connie stood.

"Carla."

"Carla." Connie smiled.

Mother bent down to kiss me on the forehead. "Kendy, go get some sun. You starting to look like white folks."

"Mother."

"I'm serious. It's a nice day. Enjoy it. I love you."

"Love you, too."

She walked out the door.

"Your mom is nice."

"Thanks. Hey, sorry about my appearance. I had a long night. I usually don't sleep this late."

Rule #1: Expect the Unexpected

"No worries. You look fine. Much better than I do when I wake up." She chuckled. "How you feeling? I been worried about you these past few days."

"Worried?" I played dumb. "About what?"

"I haven't seen you since the Crab Shack. And when I call you, it always sounds like something's wrong."

"I'm fine. I just been concentrating on school more."

"I can understand that."

I sat quietly for a moment, running my hands through my hair.

Connie softly clapped her hands to break the silence. "You want to go get something to eat? You must be starved."

"Yeah, I could use a bite."

"Me, too. After that, we can see what kind of movie is playing. Catch a matinee, maybe. Unless you have plans."

"My plans involve a pillow." I laughed. "I'd love to get out with you. What's playing?"

"There's this French flick I been dying to see. A love story, sort of."

"French? You speak French?"

"It's subtitled." She laughed. "I speak one language, like all black-blooded Americans."

"It sure the hell ain't Ebonics. With your proper behind."

We cracked up.

"Is it cold outside? Should I get my coat?"

Connie laughed out loud.

"What's so funny?" I wondered if my eagerness looked pathetic.

"Well, to answer your question: no, it's not cold, outside. But it's also not warm enough for cut-offs and a tank top."

I looked down at my makeshift pajamas. I could feel the crimson taking over my caramel complexion. Any other moment I probably would've wanted to crawl underneath a rock and hide. But when I looked at Connie's warm face, all I could do was smile. And go get decent, of course.

* * *

"You *liked* that movie?" I said from the passenger side of Connie's forest green, Ford Explorer.

"I can't believe you didn't like it. That movie was so romantic."

"He died at the end."

"But she buried him under the tree where they first met."

"If you could call kissing-naked-in-the-rain a first meeting."

"It's French." She laughed. "They invented a kiss, for Goddess sake."

"Goddess? You're a feminist?"

"Not active." She pulled into the parking lot of Dryton park. "But I'm all for women's rights."

"I heard that. And African-Amerikan rights."

"And gay rights." She parked in front of Lake Dryton. "You ready to go home? Or is this okay?"

"This is perfect. The day is perfect. Thanks for dragging me out the house." I stepped out of the car.

"Well, I couldn't let you miss a day like this. What kind of friend would I be?" She joined me in the fresh air.

"Have you ever been kayaking?"

"Like in a boat?"

I laughed. "No, on a raft. Of course, in a boat. Only it's called a kayak."

"The kind that has a hole you climb into so if you tip over, you're stuck?"

"You're afraid of water? You get to wear a life jacket."

"You'll have to take me sometime."

"Sometime soon."

"Okay. I'd risk crawling into a deathtrap to see you in one of those wet suits."

I paused, shocked.

"No, I didn't mean it like that. Not like *see* you in a wet suit. I meant because they're kind of hard to put on. From what I've seen in movies."

"Must've been one of those damned French movies."

We both laughed.

"I'm tired. You wanna sit?" I sat down on a log next to the lake. The lake was calm and the sun was about to make it's departure. The moment was perfect.

Rule #1: Expect the Unexpected

Connie joined me on the log. We sat in silence, listening to nature. Then we heard a very distinctive sound.

"Oh, oh. Don't stop."

We both stood up.

"Is somebody doing what I think they're doing?" I whispered.

"Sounds like it. Let's get out of here." she whispered back.

We started walking away until I heard his name:

"Oooh, Darius."

I wrote it off as a coincidence until I heard her name:

"Yeah, do that, Keisha."

I recognized the voice before I recognized the name. I stopped in my tracks.

"Let's go." Connie pulled my arm.

I snatched my arm from her grasp and headed towards the sound.

"No, Kendall, don't," Connie warned.

But it was too late. I had already found them.

"What the hell is this? Get the fuck up." I yelled at my friend and ex-asshole.

They weren't even naked. Her skirt was up, his zipper down, but they weren't naked.

"Kendall, let me explain," Keisha had the nerve to say. She pulled her skirt down over her big ass. Her panties were still on the grass.

Darius searched for his socks and shoes.

"It ain't what it look like."

"Keisha, I don't know what else this could be. What were you doing? Practicing Yoga?"

Darius had the nerve to chuckle.

That's when I really lost it:

"You think this shit is funny, Darius? You think you're regal because you have two women fighting over your triflin' ass? Well, I'm not fighting over you. I'm the one who let your ass go, remember? I didn't even like you. Even a fool would know that." I paused to chuckle. "But I guess I *should* consider who I'm talking to. You couldn't even get me to sleep with you. After a year, too. That's weak."

He stood up with a snarl on his face.

"You gonna hit me, again?"

"Go wait in the car, Babe," Keisha said.

Darius walked away, carrying his shoes.

Connie stood behind me, uneasily.

"Listen, Kendall. Here's what went down." Keisha placed her hand on my shoulder.

I slapped her hand away.

"One night he came over to the house lookin' for you. He seemed sad and I was here. Meeka was out with Marcus so we talked. After that, we started bein' friends. Talkin' and stuff. Mainly about you. How he was kinda hurt about you guys breakin' up."

I braced myself for the stab.

"After awhile, we started talkin' less about you and more about me."

"And let me guess," I cut in, "he cried, you consoled him, then you screwed him?"

Her eyes fluttered to the ground. The streetlight highlighted a mosquito buzzing around her head. She didn't shoo it away.

Thick puffs of smoke seeped from my nostrils. "How could you do this to me? I trusted you. I thought you were my friend."

"I *am* your friend. That's why I didn't tell you. I didn't wanna hurt you. You like my sistah. But I really like him."

"He hit me." My voice was small.

She touched my shoulder, again.

I hit her hand, again. I was seeing red. Images of my open hand making contact with her chubby cheek popped into my mind. I stood still for a minute not really knowing what to say. I mean, how could one ever be prepared to be part of some ghetto *Beverly Hill's 90210* shit? I decided to take the calm approach.

"How long has this been going on? Were you sneaking around while me and him were still together?"

"No. 'Course not. This just happened, recently. I would've never did this while you was still with him."

"I see. So you had the decency to wait until we broke up. You're a great friend after all." Calm disappeared into the lake.

Keisha put her head down.

"I can't believe you would stoop this low." I stepped closer to her. My finger was pointed only inches from her face. "I guess

Rule #1: Expect the Unexpected

I can believe it. You triflin' heifer. I should beat the crap out of you right now," my skinny behind threatened.

"Come on, let's just go." Connie grabbed my right arm which rested on my hip with ire.

I jerked my arm from Connie's grasp. "I trusted you, Keisha. Cared for you like a sistah. Who was there when you found out your own Mama stole your tuition money? Who was there when you almost got kicked out of school for cheating? Who was there when Lonnie cheated on you?" I fought back tears. "I should beat you down."

Connie grabbed my arm, again. "She's not worth it, Kendall."

"This don't have shit to do with you, Connie. So, don't be standin' your dyke ass in my face insultin' me. You don't think I know what you're up to? She's straight, Connie, so back off."

"That wasn't even called for, Keisha. Who do you think you are?" Connie held her ground.

"Connie ain't done nothing to you. You're the one who betrayed my trust. I can expect this kind of lowly shit from Darius. But you-" I stopped mid sentence, my lips trembled with rage.

Keisha lowered her head, again, pitifully.

I stepped back and folded my arms across my chest. I could feel tiny beads of perspiration forming at the base of my neck. I could feel the rage slowly filling up my lungs, inhibiting my ability to breathe comfortably.

"Look, Ken-"

"Don't ever speak my name again. As of right now, you're nothing to me. Just like you've made me nothing. Don't call me. Don't look at me. I don't even want you to think about me. You really hurt me. And right now, I hate you for it. Fortunately, I never loved Darius so I can't hate him. But I can honestly say I feel nothing but hate for you." I sighed. I felt exhausted. "Let's go, Connie."

I followed Connie to the car like a zombie. I felt as if I were in a dream. Or a nightmare, for that matter. Even though I didn't love Darius and Keisha wasn't my best friend, I still felt hurt. Even an attack from a complete stranger hurts in some way. Know what I mean?

Connie didn't say much to me on the car ride home. The only thing that could be heard was the sound of me breathing heavily, in and out.

"Call me, Kendall. If there's anything I can do-" Connie's voice trailed off in the wind as I stepped out of her car. "You sure you don't want to crash at my house, tonight? I'll leave you alone."

I responded nonverbally with a head shake.

That night, after barely touching my dinner and refusing several calls from Tomeeka and Connie, I went to bed. I started thinking about how I couldn't trust anybody. Except maybe Kiara and Mother. And God, of course. But I could trust with all my heart that the five pills I consumed earlier would rock me to sleep. I mean, what better way to deal with problems than to dream?

chapter fourteen

An Hour Late But Always on Time

Dear Reader,
    I remember when my father took off work and enrolled in mechanic school. Mother's bookstore was just taking off the ground so she was never around. I was nine-years-old and the sudden change in parental roles didn't occur to me at all. The only memory I had was coming home from school to a messy house with my father somewhere amongst all the chaos. Somehow the abnormality of the situation became lost in an unhealthy snack cake followed by a few hours of cartoons. Not having the constant guidance of a mother was pure bliss. That is, until Halloween rolled around.
    I remember Halloween being a time for hacked up sheets, face paint and unlimited sweets. That particular Halloween, I was going to be Dracula. Since Mother minored in art, I knew I was going to get the blue ribbon for the most creative costume in the school contest. But on the morning of October 31st, fate had different plans for young Kendall Reed.
    On Halloween morning, I remember waking up early and bursting into my parents room. I ran around to the right side of the bed where Mother usually slept to wake her. It was time for her to work magic on my yellow-toned face. But to my dismay, Mother wasn't there. I searched through the house and finally found a note sitting on the counter next to the Fruity Pebbles. The note was from Mother and stated that she was called into the store early and would not be able to help with my costume. She concluded that my father would paint my face. I was so upset that I couldn't eat breakfast. I sat down on the couch wearing my

black cape with my arms folded across my chest with the most vicious snarl that a nine-year-old could produce.

I remember my father walking through the door with a newspaper and coffee in his hands.

I was so upset that I couldn't even bring myself to look at him. Then, to my surprise, he placed a chair right in front of me and sat down. He grabbed the make-up from the table and began to create. Aside from fishing and watching TV together, it was the first time that my father paid one-on-one attention to me. It took all my will not to smile as he placed stroke after stroke of white, black and red make-up on my face. I couldn't wait to get to a mirror and to see his creation. When I did see my reflection, I remember smiling; there was white paint mixed with black paint, crooked lines here and there but in my mind, I was the most beautiful Dracula ever.

At school, when I received my 'participation' certificate, all I could think of was how lucky I was to have such a caring father. How, no matter what he had done to hurt me in the past, I could still count on him to come through.

And I'll be forever grateful for that.

chapter fifteen

New Beginnings

"How you been, Ken?"

"Okay. Just trying to get by. You know how it goes."

"Yeah. I ain't heard from you in awhile. I called your phone but all I got was that damn voice message."

"I never got it."

"Humph. Did you also not get the messages I left with Mother? Probably not since you always seem to be sleep these days."

"Ki, I'm on the freeway right now and my cell phone is acting up. Can I call you back later?"

"Nope, I ain't fallin' for that. Talk to me now."

I sighed. It wasn't like I was purposely trying to avoid my sister. But between school, work and trying to catch a few z's here and there, I didn't have much time for social calls. And hell, wasn't my sanity worth more than trying to please everybody and their damn mama?

"When you coming down?" she asked.

"When are *you* coming up here?"

"Wait a minute. Am I on a hidden camera show? When's the man gonna pop out of my rose bush and tell me to smile?"

"What're you talking about?" I noticed I was going ninety-mph. I decreased my speed to seventy.

"Listen to how short you are with me. Is this about Darius? 'Cause no man is worth this."

Damn. Mother had such a big mouth. The last thing I needed was a lecture from my sister. I mean, how is a woman supposed to heal when she's reminded of her wounds each and every day?

"Listen to me, Ken. I'll let you get to wherever you're going but as soon as you get there, I want you to call me." She sighed. "Have you been drinking?"

"And driving?"

"Don't get cynical. You know what I meant."

"You know how I feel about alcohol. Of course I'm not drinking. That's stupid. I'm just trying to maintain. Darius wasn't worth a dime to me, anyway."

"Yeah, I know. But something's wrong. I know my sister." She sighed, again. "You know you can talk to me, right?"

"Yeah, I know. And I will." I signaled and took the downtown exit. Traffic was thick, as usual.

"You'll call me soon as you get to where you're going?"

"I'll call you soon as I get home. I'm on my way to meet a friend." I honked my horn at an impatient driver who cut in front of me too close. "Bastard."

"You just make sure you take care of yourself. You my favorite sister."

I chuckled. "And you're mine."

"Call me."

"I will, Ki. I promise. Later."

"Later."

I flipped my cell phone closed. Although I was appreciative of everyone's concern, I was sick of people getting in my business. I mean, everybody goes through shit in their life. Why was it that every time I went through it, I had to share it with the whole damn world? I mean, so what if I had to take a pill here and there to rest. Besides, why would it be sold over-the-counter if it was so harmful? It's not like I was buying cocaine in a dark alley. Know what I mean?

* * *

"What do we say?"
"NO."
"To what?"
"TO DRUGS."
"And?"
"ALCOHOL."
"And?"

"VIOLENCE."

"And?"

"GUNS."

I watched with admiration as Connie stood in a circle holding hands with the kids of Aim High. There were about twelve kids between the ages of five and thirteen. Most of them were black but there was one or two Hispanics in the bunch. All eyes were on Connie as she led them in the chant.

I held up the wall in the back of the brightly lit room hoping to remain unnoticed until the end of the meeting.

"Hey everybody. There's a special guest here, today. Come on in, Kendall."

I took my place between Connie and a bright-eyed boy in a blue baseball cap.

"This is Kendall. She's a very good friend of mine. I want you all to make her feel welcome."

"Hi." I looked around the circle and noticed an older sistah wearing a green, Kenti cloth dress with a matching head wrap. "Sorry I'm late. Very nice place."

The walls were decorated with beautiful collaborations of pictures that seemed to speak. Musical notes and huge, colorful shapes lined the walls. There was also a mural of children with rainbow-colored faces playing together in one giant playground.

"Welcome, Kendall. You're not late. We're just starting. Before we break off into free time, we always talk about how our weeks went and what we're thankful for. I'll start," the sistah with the Kenti cloth said. She had an island accent. "My week was long. My oldest daughter is getting ready for da prom and working my nerves with all the last minute details. But overall, I'm thankful for my family."

One-by-one, the children began to speak.

"I'm thankful for my mama."

"I'm thankful for my dog."

"I'm thankful for ice-cream."

"I'm thankful that my daddy's prayers have been answered. He been sayin', 'lord please don't make me have to hit her.' And last night, I didn't have to hold the ice on mama's face."

The last comment came out of the mouth of a girl who couldn't have been a day over eight. *It only takes once for me.*

"I'm thankful for new beginnings," Connie said with a light squeeze to my hand.

"Amen," the older sistah said.

"What about you, Kendall? It's your turn."

I searched deep inside but at that moment, amidst a sea of innocent faces, I couldn't think of one thing I was grateful for. Work? No. School? No. My family? That had already been said.

"How do we reach the top?"

"Aim High," the kids yelled, at once.

Connie winked at me.

At that, all the kids broke away to find their individual areas of comfort.

"Nice to finally meet you, Kendall. I'm Ifa. Connie has told me so much about you, I feel like we're already chums," the lady with the wrap said.

"Nice to meet you, Ifa. What an amazing program you've put together."

"I'll be right back," Connie said with a squeeze to my shoulder. She began to walk around the room to mingle with the kids.

My admiration slowly turned to adoration.

"She's amazing, isn't she?" Ifa said.

"Yeah, she is." I sighed, taking in my own thoughts.

"She talks a lot about you."

"Good things, I hope."

"Let's just say, sometimes I t'ink she's talking about God."

I laughed.

"No joke."

I looked over at Connie. She was in the playhouse area pretending to flip plastic eggs.

"I sometimes worry for her," Ifa said.

"Worry?"

"Yeah, with her mama's situation, she had to grow up too fast." She adjusted her head wrap, which was starting to lean over to one side.

"Her mom's situation?"

"I've said too much, again. Con, always tells me I talk too much. My mama use to say I talk too fast. But I figure if people would listen faster, we'd be even." She chuckled. Her round belly shook as she laughed.

"I love the mural."

"It was Con's idea to paint these walls. She designed all da murals. All we had to do was paint within da lines."

"I didn't know she was an artist."

"Uh-huh. She's amazing. And she likes you, too. But I'm sure you know dat. You're much prettier than da last girl. And nicer. I'm just happy to see her smile."

"Last girl?" I stared at Ifa like she was crazy.

"I said too much, again. Let me go before I end up telling you all Con's business." She shook my hand. "Come again, Kendall."

I went over to join Connie in the playhouse area. After trying Connie's imaginary breakfast, I began to crave real food.

"Let's get out of here," Connie whispered in my ear, as if reading my mind.

In less than a second we were out the door.

"That was amazing. Thanks for inviting me," I said once we were alone. Initially, I planned on going home, taking a pill or two and getting some sleep. But since it was Saturday afternoon, Connie insisted that I join her for lunch. After lunch, I ended up at her apartment watching *Silence of The Lambs*. It was Connie's movie choice. I mean, after eating a turkey and cranberry sandwich why would I choose a movie about a sick bastard feasting on human flesh?

"Yeah, those kids are something, huh?"

"And you, too. I mean, the way you are with those kids. You're so natural."

"Yes, I think all children need a positive role model. Whether at home, school or somewhere simple as a grocery store. You know?"

I nodded my head. "You're amazing."

She smiled. "Shh. This is the best part."

I covered my eyes with the pillow right before Anthony Hopkins bit somebody's face.

"I can't believe you like that mess," I said, once the movie ended.

"A little bit of horror never hurt anybody."

"Neither have I. So why must you torture me with this crap?"
She hit me with the pillow.
I hit her back.
We started to laugh.

Then it happened; dead silence filled the room. An awkward silence that had nothing to do with fatigue. It was the kind of silence that, in the past, I always felt to be kind of cheesy. You know the moment right before a guy tries to kiss you at the end of a lame date? But Connie was a woman. She was my friend. And we damn sure weren't on no date. Well, not a romantic date, anyway. So why, after a great afternoon, was I sitting there listening to the buzz of the refrigerator and suddenly becoming aware of the pounding of my heart?

"How about some music?"

I'm not sure who spoke. All I know is suddenly Cree Summers was singing and I felt a lightheadedness that I couldn't blame on alcohol.

"Can I ask you a question?"

I didn't look Connie in the eyes as she spoke. I nodded my head since I couldn't/wouldn't find my voice.

When I look I see you in me. We don't have to fight it.

"Have you ever been in love? I mean, really in love?"

Now if it were any other person asking me about love, I probably would've told them where to go. But to Connie, I answered, "I think so."

She laughed.

I clenched my teeth.

"I'm not laughing at you. It's just that when you're in love, there's no question in your mind. You just know."

"But how do you know it's not an infatuation? How do you know you're not just in love with being in love?"

"It's just a feeling. And when it happens, you know." She stretched her legs out in front of her. We were both sitting on the carpet. "You know how when you were a teenager you thought you were in love because when he or she kissed you, your stomach turned flips?"

"Yeah, but by the next week, the feeling went away and you realized your stomach only turned because the concept of kissing was new." I suddenly felt comfortable again. Just as quickly as the awkwardness hit.

"Exactly. But when you're in love, when you're really in love, that feeling deep down in your stomach never goes away." She turned and faced me. "When you talk, laugh. Just simply being."

I avoided her eyes.

Revelation Sunshine.

"It's just something you know. You can feel it."

At that moment in time, I could feel it: a sinking feeling deep down in the pit of my stomach. Like acute nausea ready to explode. And I did explode. Right into the bleach-smelling toilet. All the contents of my lunch filled the bowl. And the rancid smell of my vomit caused me to spill my guts a second time.

"Kendall, are you okay?" Connie spoke softly through the closed bathroom door. "Can I come in?"

"No, don't come in." I flushed the toilet, watching the acidic fragments of my fear swim spherically down the drain.

"Are you okay?"

"Yeah, I'm fine. Must've been your imaginary breakfast. I'm not used to pork."

She chuckled. "You know where I am if you need anything." I collected myself from the bathroom floor, swished a capful of mouthwash around my gums then rejoined Connie in the living room.

Cree Summers was no longer playing on the stereo. In fact, no sound could be heard except for the sound of the refrigerator motor.

"I think I better call it a night."

"You sure? I have some herbal tea that might do the trick."

"I promised my sister I'd call her."

"You can call her here." She paused and looked down at her watch. "It's eight. I'd feel better knowing you weren't out driving sick. Stay here."

"Maybe I'll just lay my head down awhile." I plopped down on the couch.

"I'd like that." She smiled.

That evening, with a cold towel placed on my forehead and a giant T-Shirt on my back, I closed my eyes. And with Connie by my side, I rested peacefully without the help of any medicinal aids.

For one night, anyway.

chapter sixteen

Stay in Your Place

"Kendall, you have a lot of potential. I think if you applied yourself more the results would be phenomenal. Let's take your paper on *carpe diem* for example."

"What about my paper?"

"How long did it take you to write it?"

"I worked on that paper for almost three days." I wasn't bullshitting either. Okay, maybe I sat down in front of the computer for two nights and ended up playing solitaire and free cell. But on the third night, I worked on that paper for a good two hours. Well, maybe an hour and a half. But that's a long time for a four-page paper. Don't you think?

"I've seen your work. I know you're capable of doing better. That's why I'm giving this paper a 'D-'." Professor Johnston handed me the paper with the offending grade written in red ink.

"A 'D-?' I've never gotten anything lower than an 'B' on a paper. I'm even better at writing than science."

"I know, Kendall. That's why I'm giving you the grade."

"But why?"

"Because the assignment was to define *carpe diem* and to relate it to a personal experience."

"So?"

"So, you gave me the definition of what it means to 'seize the day'. But you didn't give any examples of writers who used this theme. You *do* have the assignment sheet, don't you?"

"Yeah." I hung my head down in shame. I thought back to the night I'd written the paper; I had taken four sleeping pills before I even remembered the paper was due. After writing one paragraph, I felt so drowsy I bullshitted my way through the other three and a half pages.

"There's a way to redeem yourself, Kendall. In fact, that's why I called you into my office."

I sat forward in my seat.

"You've heard of the Black Hole, haven't you?"

"The literary magazine here at Dry U?"

"Yes. I'm the chief editor and would like for you to submit a piece. Based on your previous work, I think you have a good chance at being chosen."

"Really?"

"Yes, really. In all my years of teaching here at Dryton, I've never met a freshman with more talent."

I blushed.

"If your piece gets selected, I'll give you full credit on your *carpe diem* paper."

"Wow. Thanks a lot, Ms. Johnston. I'll do my best."

"I know you will, Kendall. Here are the guidelines."

"Thanks." I stood up and grabbed the piece of paper. "Have a nice day."

"You, too. Good luck."

I walked out of the office with a smile on my face. I never knew I had talent. Even though I felt the most alive when writing in my journal.

Connie was waiting for me outside Professor Johnston's office.

"What took you so long? Are you in trouble?"

"Not exactly." I relayed the entire conversation from A to Z and handed her the guidelines.

"Are you kidding me? What are you going to write? Or have you already written it? I've heard that true writers can write in their dreams. Is that true?"

I laughed. "Whoa, Tiger. I still have to submit my piece. Who knows if it'll even get picked."

"It will."

"Thanks." I smiled.

She blushed.

"You done for the day?"

"Yes. You want to get something to eat?"

"I could use a bite or two. I need to stop home first and

Stay in Your Place

change into some shorts." I was sweating like a South Carolina slave in my blue jeans and black, T-Shirt.

"Should we just meet somewhere?"

"I'll meet you at your apartment in about thirty minutes."

"Until then."

* * *

I knew something was up the moment I pulled up to the house; Kiara's black Lexus was parked in front as well as Mother's green Volvo. My heart was beating a thousand times per minute as I walked through the door.

"Hey, Ken. Where the hell you been?"

I could tell by the enthusiasm in Kiara's voice that everything was okay.

"I was at school. Getting my edu-ma-cation."

We hugged.

"Where's Mother?"

"She back there shootin' up, again."

"Did she eat first?" 'Shooting up' is a term that Kiara and I came up with to make light of Mother's diabetes, an otherwise traumatic situation.

"Yeah, we just had lunch, *Dr. Reed.*" Kiara joked.

"You stupid." I lightly slapped her shoulder. "What you doing here? Out of the blue?"

"That's what I been asking her for the past hour." Mother joined us with an empty insulin syringe in her hand. She tossed the needle into the 'sharps' container.

"Hey, Mother." I kissed her cheek.

"I wanted you both here at the same time. That way I don't have to go through it twice," Kiara said.

"Go through what twice? And what about Daddy?" I asked.

"It's girl talk," Kiara said.

"Then, are you gonna spit it out or what?" I said.

"When the time is right," Kiara teased.

We all sat around in the living room. I looked down at my watch. A half hour had already passed. I needed to call Connie. "I'll be right *black.*"

"Where you think you're, goin'?"

"Back to my room, if that's okay with you, *Queen* Kiara."

"Uh-uh, Missy. You not that grown, yet."

"I have to make a phone call. Is that alright with you?"

"Why can't you use the phone, right there?" Kiara pointed to the cordless phone, in the kitchen.

I blushed.

"You dating already? This soon?" She smiled. "I heard that."

"No, it ain't like that. I'm just calling a friend."

"Male?"

"Female."

"Female?" Kiara dramatically placed her hand on her chest.

"It's her new friend, Connie." Mother saved the day. "She's a nice girl."

"Good. I don't like those ghetto friends she used to hang around. You know the big one and the one with the air-brushed toenails? I hate airbrush."

Mother laughed.

I left them to their conversation and went to call Connie. When I returned, Mother and Kiara were talking about the Darius breakup. Luckily, I hadn't updated them about Keisha and Darius.

"You get a hold of her, Kendy?" Mother asked.

"Yeah, she's coming over in fifteen minutes to meet Kiara." I sat down on the couch. "Why you guys talking about ancient herstory? Forget about Darius."

"Why you gotta get all feminist on us?"

I threw a couch pillow at Kiara. "So, what's up, Ki? Not that I'm complaining, but what you doing here in the middle of the week?"

"Okay, you ready for this?"

Mother leaned forward in her seat.

"For God's sake, tell us already," I blurted out.

"Okay, okay." She cleared her throat. "Mother. Kendall. Tim and I are gonna have a baby. I mean, I'm pregnant."

Mother and I cheered.

It was so noisy in the Reed house that you'd have thought someone won the lottery. Scratch that; a new addition to the

Reed family was better than splitting ten million dollars with five other winners. Know what I mean?

After the cheering, the questions began.

I asked:

"How many months are you?"

"Three."

Mother asked:

"You feeling okay? You getting morning sickness, yet?"

"Morning sickness. Afternoon sickness. Evening sickness."

Like an idiot, I asked:

"Does Tim know?"

"Know? He's the one who planned it."

Then, Mother had the nerve to ask:

"You sure you ready? I mean, financially?"

"Of course, Mother. Otherwise we wouldn't have planned it."

"Yeah, I know. Just making sure."

Kiara exhaled. "Dang, you guys are asking more questions than when I told Tim's mom."

A whole new set of questions came out, then.

"What about his drug-addict father? You not gonna bring the baby around that mess, are you? And ain't Tim's mama always mean to you? What's she gonna do when the baby gets here? I'm not letting nobody mistreat my first grandchild." Mother paused for a quick breath of air. "My first grandchild. My baby's having a baby."

The tears came next. From Mother and Kiara, anyway. I've never been one for waterworks. So all I could do was run and get my camera.

"Stop crying for just a second and say, 'cheese'."

They both turned and faced the camera.

"Can I take pictures of the birth?"

"Right now, I'll say okay. But who knows what I'm gonna be saying when I'm on that table screaming bloody murder."

"I heard that." Mother gave Kiara five. "I'm gonna be a Grandma. Wait'll I tell Mama. Wait'll I tell my sisters. And my staff. Oh, honey, this is one of the happiest days of my life."

I looked at the glow in Mother's eyes and I couldn't help but feel jealous. It's not like I wasn't ever planning on having children. It's just that, I could never picture myself playing wife and mother to a husband and some kids. So if my biological clock were to tick, I'd just get some eligible bachelor to fertilize me. But then again, all this was coming from a girl who's never been mentally attracted to a guy. And the one guy I gave the time of day to was abusive. So, maybe I was thinking out of the side of my neck. But all I know is I wanted Mother to be looking at me with the same glow she dedicated to Kiara.

The doorbell rang.

"Hey, Connie," I leaned forward and whispered in her ear, "thank *God* you're here."

She looked at me, quizzically.

"I'll tell you, later," I whispered.

"Connie. Come on in, Baby," Mother said.

"So this is the infamous Connie."

I shot Kiara a warning glare but she continued, anyway.

"Since Kendall ain't got no manners at all, allow me to introduce my damn self."

"Kiara where my belt? Don't think 'cause your house is bigger than mine, you can come over here and act grown. Like I always tell Kendy, you ain't too old to get a whoopin'."

"Come on, Mother. That slipped out. I don't be cussin'." Kiara winked at me.

"Don't worry, Connie, we're just all so happy to see each other," Mother said.

Connie laughed. "Don't mind me. It just makes me long for the sister I never had."

"You can be our sister." Kiara smiled. "But I'll always be the prettiest one. Remember that."

"And now you're the fattest one," I said with a smile.

Connie looked alarmed.

"She's pregnant," Mother said, beaming.

"Yes, I'm pregnant." Kiara rolled her eyes and faced me. "And since I'm eating for two, you can buy me lunch, Smart Ass."

"Kiara."

"Sorry, Mother. But you know how moody the expecting can get?"

"Ain't that the truth." Mother sighed. "We just ate, Kiara."

"That burger is floating somewhere in sewage world."

I opened the front door. "Let's get out of here before you embarrass me more," I said to Kiara.

Connie softly grabbed my arm.

I blushed.

"Chinese okay?" Mother asked.

Kiara ran to the bathroom.

* * *

"I told his little mannish self to keep it in his pants."

"Or at least cover it up every once in awhile."

"He had the nerve to say it don't feel right wearing a condom."

Mother, Kiara, Connie and I were sitting up at Heavy's Tex Mex, a little Americanized-Mexican food joint in downtown Dryton. Connie and I were munching on chicken burritos while Mother and Kiara were gossiping, as usual. The subject, this time, was my oldest cousin Ryan. Apparently, some little nappy-haired girl he's been running around with turned up pregnant. According to Ryan, he's in love and wants to start a family. All of this sounds okay except for the fact that both of them are still in high school. Babies making babies has turned from an epidemic to a reason for guerrilla warfare. Know what I mean?

"Neither of them have a pot to piss in nor a window to throw it out."

"Mother, you and those old phrases." Kiara took a sip of her lemon-lime soda.

Kiara and Mother were the only ones talking; I've always made it a point not to gossip, too much. I mean, I wouldn't want somebody to be blabbing my business all over town. Although, I'm sure they would if I had some.

"What does, Lorraine think about all this?" Kiara asked.

Lorraine is the third oldest female in the Jensen clan. Dottie and Harvey Jensen, are the proud parents of five girls, five boys, about thirty grandchildren and two soon-to-be great grandchildren. Just one big, ghetto family.

"Who knows?" Mother bit into a salsa-dipped chip. "But she's probably too busy being worried about that fast daughter of hers."

"What's Renee up to these days?" I climbed into the gossip.

"Exactly nothing," Mother answered.

"At least she's in school. You have to give her credit for that," Kiara said.

"That's true, even if she is only taking one class."

"One class?" Kiara and I said at the same time.

"It's better than nothing." I pushed my plate back.

"Weight training, though?" Mother said.

We all cracked up. I mean, the great thing about higher learning is you get to set your own pace. But weight training?

"Connie, what's your major?" Kiara asked.

"English." She bit into her burrito.

"I heard that. What you wanna do? Teach?"

"I thought about teaching. But mainly I want to publish."

"Well, we need more sistahs and brothahs marketing books. It's hard for *us* to break through to such a white, male-dominated business. You know what I'm saying?" Mother said.

"Yes, that's why I want to start my own company. Break into the industry. There are too many brilliant voices that remain unheard because the market has turned so commercial, you know?" Connie pushed back her plate.

"Yeah, I know. That's why, at my store, I don't have a separate African-Amerikan section."

"Mother, that's because your entire store is African-Amerikan," I said.

"Darn right it is. I was sick and tired of going into those big, two-story chain stores and finding one shelf dedicated to African-American literature."

"Yes, as if Black literature's not considered American." Connie leaned forward with her elbows on the table.

"Kind of like saying, 'you can join us as long as you stay in your place'," Mother said.

We all slapped hands across the table.

"Kendy used to write all the time."

"Mother." I shot her a warning glance.

"Yeah, I remember all those poems you used to jot down in like a matter of seconds." Kiara smiled at me. "I used to steal them and pretend I wrote them. I gave some of them to Tim."

Stay in Your Place

I laughed. "I guess I grew out of it."

"Or maybe you just need to wait for the right inspiration to come along." Connie smiled at me.

I blushed.

"Did you see that?" Mother said.

"What?" I jumped. Did she see me blush?

"Those two women all hugged up like they a man and woman." Mother pointed outside at two young women face-to-face in a loving embrace.

To me, it was beautiful.

"Relax, Mother. It's not like you ain't never been to the Bay."

"We ain't in the Bay, Kiara. This is Dryton. We not ready for that mess."

I sighed. I knew it was matter of time before Mother said something to embarrass me. I didn't want Connie to think Mother was a bigot.

"I'm stuffed." I tried to change the subject as quickly as possible.

Connie picked at her burrito.

"My best friend tried to call herself switching sides," Mother continued.

"Becky?" Kiara asked.

"Yeah. After her husband left she called herself fed up with men. Now she's living with a woman. But I told her I wasn't gonna have no part of her lifestyle."

"You ended your friendship because she fell in love?"

"I didn't end the friendship, Kiara. I just told her not to bring that mess around me, that's all." Mother took a sip of her iced tea. "She can still come over as long as she don't rub that girlfriend mess in my face."

"You can join me as long as you stay in your place." I threw in my two cents.

Connie and Kiara laughed.

Mother was fuming. "You know it ain't the same thing. Being black and being gay is two different things."

"What about being black *and* gay?" Kiara asked.

We all laughed.

Except for Mother, of course. "When I walk into a store, people know right away, I'm black. I have no choice. But it's they own choice to walk into that store gay."

"Mother, that's ridiculous. Comparing race to sexual orientation is like comparing peaches to pears." Kiara paused to suck some salsa off her chip, then dipped it back into the bowl. "Yes, we're black. And everybody in this restaurant knows we're all black at this table. But nobody knows who we love. That's our business. The only people that should care are the two people involved in the love."

Connie smiled.

I squirmed in my seat.

"Don't think you got the last word, Kiara. I'm still entitled to my own opinion. And if it makes me uncomfortable, I don't have to be around it. Conversation over." Mother motioned to the waiter for the check.

"Okay, Mother, you win. And for your prize, you get to foot the bill," Kiara said.

Even Mother had to laugh at that one.

chapter seventeen

Acquired Taste

She said she would pick me up by seven. Instead, she showed up at six forty-five. I wasn't even finished getting dressed. Well, I was almost dressed but couldn't decided whether to wear the black fitted pants with the white button-up or the loose pin-stripped pants with the black silk blouse. Black boots with the heal or without? Hair up or down? Damn, I couldn't remember ever feeling so flustered. I mean, it wasn't like I was going out on a date or anything.

"Kendall, I'm sending Connie back, okay?"

I couldn't let Connie see me half naked. I decided on the black fitted pants with a wine-colored blouse. Hell, it's not often that the "Phantom of The Opera" hits a small venue like the Dryton Civic Auditorium.

"Mother wait. I'm not dressed." I poked my head out the door. Connie was standing in the hallway dressed to the nines in a dark-brown, two-piece pants suit with a sleeveless jacket. Her hair hung loosely in ringlets around her shoulders.

"I'll be only two minutes, I promise." I couldn't let her in my room. I couldn't let her see the mess I'd created with my nervousness.

"You need help, Kendy?" Mother started to open the door.

"I'll be right out. Mother, please." I blocked the door with my foot.

"Ain't got but a minute of meat on those bones but you wanna take an hour to get dressed."

"It's okay, Mrs. Reed. We have time. I'm thirsty, anyway."

"What a nice girl. It's Carla, remember? Come on in the kitchen, Connie. You hungry? I made some chicken, macaroni and cabbage. You hurry up now, Kendy."

Connie turned and winked as she and Mother disappeared down the hall.

Just as I finished putting the finishing touches on my hair, the phone rang.

"Kendall?"

"Hey, Tomeeka."

"I guess I can call the police then."

"What?" I didn't have time to hear about her and Marcus' bullshit.

"I guess I can call the police and tell them you ain't missin' after all."

"Nope, I'm right here. How you been?" I stepped into my black, heeled boots.

"I'm okay. I been wonderin' about you, though. You don't return my calls no more. You still mad at me?"

"I was never mad at you. Just irritated."

"I wanted to tell you 'bout Keisha and Darius. You know I did."

"Yeah, I know you did. But you still should've told me. A *real* friend would've told me." I cut her deep.

"I'm sorry." She sighed.

"But anyways."

"Yeah, anyways. How's school goin'?"

"Good. You know chemistry can kick a girl's ass."

"I don't know how you do it. That's why I'ma stick to the remedial edges for as long as I can. But next semester I have to take a science course."

"Oh, yeah the nursing thing." I gave myself the once over in my full-length mirror. "Hey, Meeka. I gotta go."

"The nursing thing? Damn, Kendy, you make it sound like it's a hobby. Why you puttin' me on the back burner? I thought you said you was gonna be here for me?"

"What're you talking about? I'm here for you. But tonight, I'm going out."

"With Connie, no doubt. You been seein' a lot of her, lately. You not switchin' sides on me, are you?"

"Switching sides? What the hell's that supposed to mean?"

"Just what I said. You know Connie's reputation around campus."

"Reputation? What is this high school? Unlike you, some of us go to school to get an education."

"I'll ignore that comment. But let's just say the whole time I've known Connie, she ain't never been with a dude. And now look at all the time she's demandin' of you."

"She's not demanding anything. I choose to be with Connie."

"Exactly. You choose to *be* with Connie. Like I said before, you switchin-"

Click. I hung up in her face. I didn't have time to be listening to Tomeeka's mess. Anyway, Connie would've told me if she was gay. I shrugged the idea off and gathered my demeanor to make the grand entrance into the living room.

"Oooo-weee, looks like somebody just stepped right outta *Jet.*"

"Mother." I blushed.

Connie looked at me and grinned.

"Both you girls are sharp as a tack. Men aren't gonna be able to keep their eyes off you."

Men were nowhere on our minds.

* * *

"That was fantastic. I've never seen anything so amazing."

After the show, Connie and I stopped off at a little cafe' in downtown Dryton. The ambiance was perfect; the lights were dim, piano music filled the overhead and I was digging into the most delicious slice of cheesecake mankind had to offer.

"That was my third time seeing 'Phantom.' Seems to get better every time. The special effects were awesome." I took a sip of my cappuccino.

"Yes. And the actress who played Christine had the most beautiful voice I've ever heard. Like being made love to for the first time."

"So is this cheesecake." I laughed. "Or so I've been told."

"You mean, you've never?"

"Never. But let's not even go there, okay?"

"Of course not." She smiled sympathetically. "I wouldn't even think of going there."

"Well, look what the cat drug up in here."

"Hey, Tomeeka. Hey Marcus." I vomited my words.

"You didn't think I was gonna let you off that easy, did you?" Tomeeka's voice cut harshly through the serene atmosphere.

"Look, can we talk about this later? This isn't the time or place." I spoke quietly but forceful.

"No need to talk later. I was outta line. I'm sorry. Can we start over?"

I nodded my head. "How'd you know I was here?"

"Your mom told me. Mind if we join ya'll?"

Connie took a sip of her caramel macchiato.

"We was about to leave. I've got work in the morning." I lied.

"You still got cheesecake on your plate," Tomeeka said. She and Marcus pulled two chairs from a nearby table and sat down.

Since most of the customers were post theatre people, Marcus and Tomeeka stuck out like two raisins in a bowl of milk.

Marcus was dressed in a navy blue, mechanic jumpsuit with a blue bandana hanging from his left pocket. As always, his hair was in cornrows and his face sported a permanent sneer.

"Marcus, ain't you gonna say 'hi' to Kendall?"

"Sup," Marcus said without even looking me in the eye.

"Hi." I looked at Connie and mouthed, "I'm sorry," when no one else was looking.

"Where's the waiter? I want one of them 'spresso dranks. What you drankin', Kendy?"

"A cappuccino." I did what I could to finish my cheesecake. But you know how hard it is to swallow something so rich.

"What brings you two out here at this time of night?" Connie asked.

"We was sittin' at the house bored and thought we'd go visit Kendall. But Mrs. Reed said she was here with you. So, here we are." Tomeeka smiled.

I suddenly began to feel like an asshole. I mean, before I met Connie, Tomeeka was always there for me. And even if she wasn't the most articulate girl in the world, she was my friend. The least I could do was treat her like a human being. Know what I mean?

"If this is your first time drinking espresso, I'd suggest something sweet. Connie is drinking a caramel macchiato. It has vanilla and caramel," I said.

"Is it good, Connie?" Tomeeka asked.

"Really good."

"Marcus, go order us what Connie has." Tomeeka smiled.

Marcus didn't even respond. He just sat back in his chair sneering.

"Baby, come on, please."

"I ain't drinking that shit, Meek." Marcus spoke above a whisper.

"Come on. You never do what I wanna do."

"Fuck this. I gotta meet my boys soon. I don't have time for this shit. Let's go."

"We just got here, Marcus. Don't embarrass me in front of my friends."

"I don't care who the fuck's around."

A nearby couple turned and glanced in our direction.

Connie slid down in her seat.

I finished up the last of my cheesecake. I knew it was only a matter of minutes before Marcus started acting a fool.

"What'd I do, Marcus?" Tomeeka started to cry.

"Let's step." Marcus stood up.

"Right now?"

"Did I stutter? Now."

"Bye, Kendall. Bye Connie. Sorry about this." Her eyes were filled with tears.

"I'm sorry," I whispered in her ear. "You wanna come home with me?"

"No, I'll be okay."

"I'll call you when I get home, okay?"

"Okay," she said. Then she hurried out the door behind Marcus' sorry ass.

Connie and I followed not too far behind.

* * *

"Is he always like that?" Connie asked once we were safe inside her SUV.

"Pretty much. He's a prick, huh?"

"To say the least. And he's the father of her baby?"

"Yeah. How'd you know she's pregnant?"

"Everybody knows. She used to wear halter tops. Now she's wearing oversized baseball jerseys." She merged onto the freeway. "It's kind of obvious."

"Yeah, I guess so. I wonder if she's told him yet." I felt like even more of an asshole for not staying in touch with my distressed friend.

"He hits her, huh?"

I nodded my head.

"I feel sorry for the child because that's who suffers when parent's fight."

"Yeah, I imagine so." I turned the radio on the slow rhythm and blues station.

"It messed my brother up."

"Your parents used to fight?"

"Non stop. Todd and I used to hide underneath the covers every time my father came home from work."

"Why? Was he abusive to you guys, too?"

"No. But by the time he came home from work, we were already in bed. Mom used to wait up for him, then yell at him over his cold dinner."

"If he was working late, why would your mom wait up?"

"Well, I don't think he was really at work. I mean, he worked, but when he came home, he smelled like alcohol." She paused to exit the freeway. "The yelling would go on back and forth for several minutes. Then the loud banging would begin."

"That's horrible."

"Tell me about it. Dishes, knives, even lamps were thrown. The sounds of Mom crying would follow shortly after."

I held my breath.

"After the fighting, Todd and I would wait."

"For what?"

"For either Papa to storm out of the house or for the loud moans of their twisted lovemaking."

"That's disgusting."

"I can't tell you what I hated more, the sounds of anger or the sounds of passion. I promised myself I'd be a virgin, forever." She pulled into my parent's driveway and turned off the engine. "But I was never good at sticking to promises."

I laughed even though nothing was really funny. "How'd it mess up your brother?"

"He turned out passive around women. Let's them walk all over him. His girlfriend cheats on him all the time. She has two kids that aren't his. All she does is take his money."

"That's horrible." I sat back in my seat. "What about you? Did you learn from it?"

"I learned from it, alright. Grew up too quick. But I think I prevailed in the end."

"I'll say. You're amazing. All your strength and courage-"

"Kendall, are you taking sleeping pills?"

"What?" Her question hit me like a brick.

"Come on, Kendall. We've known each other long enough. And I think we've developed quite a good friendship. Don't you?"

"Yeah, but that still don't mean you can just sit there and ask me personal questions-"

"Please answer me."

"Yeah, I do. Occasionally when I can't sleep."

"I suspected it when I picked you up for the movie."

"It's a legal drug. I buy them over-the-counter." I unlatched my seatbelt.

"People still get addicted to them."

"What a way to end a good evening. Go right ahead and turn nothing into something. I'm a grown ass woman. I know what I'm doing."

"Calm down, Kendall. I'm not trying to interrogate you. I'm concerned about you. I know what addictions can do to people. I've seen it happen."

"I'm not addicted. I just had a few sleepless nights. Damn."

"I didn't say you were addicted. Just let me finish my story." She rested both hands on the steering wheel. "When my father left us, Mom didn't know what to do. We lived in the suburbs but Mom didn't work. She did what too many women fall victim to in marriages; she relied solely on her husband for financial support."

"So what did you guys do?" I relaxed.

"Well, fortunately, the house was in both my parent's names. So Mom hired a lawyer and took Papa to court. He was a no-show, so we were able to keep the house." She paused, briefly. "But as the months went by, she discovered that she didn't have the education or experience to get a decent job. So, she ended up having to sell the house."

"At least you weren't left with nothing."

"Kendall, my mom and dad lived in that house together for fifteen years. She was devastated enough when he left her. Having to sell the house was like opening a wound that never had the chance to heal in the first place."

"That's awful." I turned my upper body towards her.

"So with money in the bank, a rented apartment, two kids and no man, Mom decided to take the easy way out."

"What'd she do?"

"She turned to legal drugs."

"Sleeping pills?" I directed the question more to myself than to Connie.

"Yes, sleeping pills. She started out just taking them a few nights a week to get over anxiety. Then she increased her habit to every night. After only a few months, she started taking sleeping pills several times a day. Pretty soon, Todd and I hardly ever saw Mom awake. It got to the point where we were forced to raise ourselves." She paused, sucking in a mouthful of air.

"Damn, Connie. Did she ever quit?"

"Eventually. But not until after Todd enlisted and I went to college. I guess she never realized she had a problem."

I shook my head and sighed. Then Connie said something I'll never forget:

"I think people with chemical addictions, whether it be illegal drugs, legal drugs or alcohol, get to the point where all the good is sucked out of life as they perceive it. They turn to these addictions as a means of escape. And the only way for them to overcome these addictions is to find something or someone worth living for and hold on to that feeling. As human beings we sometimes allow the bad to subconsciously wash out the good. We tend to forget about the little things in life that make us happy."

After Connie finished talking, all I could do was sit back and think about everything. Was I starting to forget about the things that used to make me smile? There was a time in my life, when the mere presence of the sun would make me smile. When just feeling the warmth of the sun caress my face was enough to keep me going throughout the day. I wondered what I could do to experience the warmth of the sun on my face, again.

I felt a few stray tears escape my eyes and stream down my cheek.

"It's okay to cry, Kendall. I didn't mean to sound harsh. I just really care about you and don't want to see you go down the same path my mom did. Trust me. It's not an appealing lifestyle for anybody."

I started thinking about Daddy and how I judged him based on his addiction. I felt guilty for condemning him based on his weakness.

Connie leaned forward and hugged me.

The instant I felt her sincere warmth showering my cold body, I had no choice but to let it all out. I started to cry. Not a silent, inward cry that most people perform when in the presence of another being. I began to sob loudly with a downpour of salty tears that poured out of every cavity on my face.

Connie continued to hug me tight while intermittently whispering soothing words of comfort.

After the tears, I sat back in my seat, concentrating on the dashboard in front of me. No words were being spoken between us but a lot was being said.

She was the first to speak. "Look, I'm sorry for the way I ended this night. I was concerned but I never meant to make you cry."

"It wasn't you who made me cry. But it *was* you who opened my eyes. Thank you." I reached for her.

The moment our bodies touched, I knew I could never turn back.

It all seemed to happen in hyper speed. You know the fine moments in life that end up turning into a vague memory? As if you were a mere observer in a special moment that belonged to someone else?

I closed my eyes to momentarily stop the haze that was starting to cloud my brain.

As if by accident, her lips brushed against my ear lobes.

And then:

Her lips began to graze my neck.

I involuntarily shivered at the warm feeling of her breath so close to my neck. I closed my eyes and took in the moment;

the feeling of closeness without any words being spoken; the feeling of intimacy without the presence of a persistent tongue or a clumsy stroke. But Connie was a woman. So why was I experiencing the same feelings I've read about so often? I felt alive and free. But the thought of being attracted to a woman terrified me. I opened my eyes and pulled myself from her embrace.

"I should go now." I opened the door and jumped out as fast as I could.

"Kendall, wait." She stopped me just as I unlocked my parents front door.

I turned and faced her, carefully avoiding her eyes.

"I'm sorry about what just happened. I took it too far."

"What're you talking about?" I kept my eyes on the pavement.

"Exactly. It was nothing." She lifted my chin with her right hand and found my eyes. "Unless, you want it to be."

"I gotta go." I practically closed the door in her face.

Mother was waiting for me on the couch. "Was that Connie? Why didn't she come in and say, 'hi'? Why you breathing so hard? Was the show good?"

I answered Mother the best I could before disappearing into the safety of my confines. I popped four pills into my mouth and let the magic begin. I pulled out my journal and began to write. Between the lines of my lyrical content, the familiar haze I experienced with Connie, began to intertwine with my pen. Somewhere in the midst, a poem was born:

Acquired Taste- Dedicated to the me I tried to ignore

Matching bodies entwined as one
Soft as silk,
The essence of a poem.
A magical embrace created by the mind,
True love enhanced by the images of time.
Intense passion.
Desire remains fought.
Negative vibes.
Desire remains untaught.
Hard Bodies rejected.
An acquired taste.
Soft and firm.
An acquired taste.
Matching souls revealing their fate.
Imprisoned by society
Through love and hate.
A soft shoulder, inviting to my tears,
Whispering words only two can hear.
Soft caresses from hands like my own.
Soft, chocolate kisses from lips
Like my own.
Interchanging thoughts,
Aligned through gender.
Electric beauty. Angelic and tender.
We are as one, body and soul.
The beginning and end.
You make me whole.
Kendall Renee' Reed

chapter eighteen

Mint Chocolate

I spent all day Sunday helping out at Mother's bookstore, *A Place Away From Home*. Fifteen years ago, when Mother first opened her bookstore, her intention was to create a legacy that Kiara and I could share with her. And even though Kiara moved away and I started pre-med, we still did what we could to keep Mother's business thriving. It was Kiara's idea to include a small cafe that offered espresso as well as milk and cookies for the little ones. And I was the one who threw in the input about starting a colorfully-matted, bean-bag-filled children's corner.

Mother's store really was a place away from home. Adults could enjoy a nice massage or pedicure in a Zen-oriented setting. With soft music playing and aromatic oils burning, most people ended up staying until closing.

"I thought you were supposed to be helping me, today."

"I am, Mother." I didn't even bother to take the book off my face as I spoke. I was laying up in a leather recliner listening to the sounds of the rain forest.

"Well, when you get off your behind, do you mind running the cafe for a minute?"

"A minute?" I finally took the book off my face and sat up. My hair was all over my head.

"Okay, maybe an hour. Janis is going home, sick." Mother smoothed down my hair.

"But you know how bad I can tear up that espresso machine. People always complain when I make coffee."

"Hey. We own this shop. Who cares what people say. And it's just this once, Kendy. For your Mother." She gave me her irresistible pout.

"Are there anymore clean aprons?" I sighed.

"That's my girl."

I was hating life by the time the third kid ran up to the counter without an adult. No adult almost always equals no money. I wasn't trying to be tyrant-like but business is business. Know what I mean? Besides, after everything that happened with Connie, my patience was running too thin. I wanted to call her but at the same time, I never wanted to hear her voice, again. Well, maybe not ever again. But at least not for a few days. I needed some time to think and get myself together.

"Can I get a large non-fat, iced, no whip, mint latte', please?" A familiar-looking sistah with silver locks interrupted my thoughts.

"Certainly. What size can I get for you?"

"Girl, don't cha know who I am?"

I squinted my eyes. "Ifa?"

"Probably didn't recognize me without my head wrap."

I smiled. "How's everything?"

"Grand like da opera. My daughter finally picked out her dress."

"Oh yeah, the prom. I remember what that was like."

"Remember? Couldn't have been more than a few months ago for you."

I laughed and grabbed a twenty-ounce paper cup. *How many shots of espresso are in a large?*

"I didn't know you worked here. I thought you did somet'ing with animals?"

"I do. I'm only helping out moms, today." I found the 'on' switch to the espresso machine and grabbed three shot glasses.

"Helping out? Your mom owns da shop? Carla Reed?"

"Yeah. Did you say non-fat?"

"Yes, Dear. You sure you know how to work dat t'ing?"

"I'm sure." Espresso began to overflow from my shot glass. "Damn, I guess I don't."

"Mind if I come 'round?"

"Help yourself." I handed her an apron.

With expertise, Ifa turned off the machine and poured non-fat milk into her cup of ice.

I leaned against the back counter.

"How's Connie?" She added three shots of espresso to her cup.

"How would I know? What's that supposed to mean?" I answered quickly. Too quickly.

"Calm your nerves, Child. You'll have a heart attack by age thirty." She added a shot of mint syrup then placed on a domed lid.

"Sorry. I guess I'm a little defensive."

"A little? You were 'bout ready to bite my head off. And after I saved your behind from making a mess back here."

I laughed. "Thanks, Ifa. You used to work at a coffee house, or something?"

"Or somet'ing is right. I've done a little bit of this, a little more of dat. When you're an immigrant in the states, you do what you will to survive."

"Where you from?"

"Grenada. You know the West Indies?"

"Yeah, Mon'," I joked.

Ifa laughed. "Don't hurt yourself, Child." She sipped her latte'.

"Do you ever think of going back there? To Grenada?"

"All the time. I visited my family, last year. But you know how they say, 'you can never go back home'?"

I grabbed an apple juice from the refrigerated display window.

"When I went back, I was frowned upon by the natives. Said I was stuck up with my California accent and all. As if I didn't shed blood, sweat and tears on Grenada soil like my forefathers."

I listened half-heartedly even though my full thoughts were on Connie. I wondered what she was thinking? I wondered if she was laying on her couch listening to slow jams and thinking about me. Then I started picturing her crying tears. Tears that I created.

"You miss her, huh?"

"What do you mean?" I stood up erect.

"You know what I mean. You can't fool Ifa."

"I don't know what you're talking about."

"You do too know what I'm talking about. I see it in your eyes. I see it in her eyes, too."

I looked around for Mother. I didn't want her to hear Ifa's mess.

"Let me tell you a story."

"I have to get back to work."

"Work? I'm your only customer, right now. And I know as a business woman, your mom taught you dat customers come first." She slurped her latte'. "Besides, da way you work dat espresso machine, I don't t'ink you'll be making sales no time soon."

I had to laugh.

"Anyway, let me take you back to da sixties. A young, hot Grenada woman in her early twenties on top of the world."

"Go on with your bad self." I slapped her hands.

"Back when I was in my prime, I felt invincible. I had dis great plan about how I was gonna come to the states, earn my degree in English and write the greatest Grenada story ever told. I had it all figured out. Or so I thought at da time. But when I got to Los Angeles, Jim Crow was my welcome mat. I started working days at a window-glass factory and nights as a waitress of a 'whites only' pub just to make ends meet. Of course school was out of da question."

"If it was a white's only establishment, how'd you get to work there?"

"Because I was a black piece of ass with a sexy accent. Pardon my French. I worked like a slave for no tips and degrading advances made by white, male pigs. And da advances were not only verbal."

"Assholes."

"It gets worse. One night, after a night of hell, a greasy, fat white man full of da devil's water, pulled me down on his lap."

I crossed my arms and rolled my eyes.

"All his friends were laughing and egging him on as he started bouncing me around on his lap and moaning obscenities in my ear."

"That's disgusting."

"And da jerk had the nerve to be aroused by my humiliation."

"You should've hit him with your serving tray."

"It was da sixties. Martin and Malcolm were fighting but da battle was far from being won." She ran her fingers over her silver locks. "Just as I started to feel like less of a human being, a tall stranger grabbed my hand and pulled me to my feet. I swear I could hear da knight in shining armor music playing in da background as my savior punched da bastard in da jaw."

"That was heroic. Especially in the sixties. Was he white?"

"Yes, he was. And he walked me outside as everyone, including the owner of da bar, called him everything from 'nigger-lover' to 'dog-lover'."

"That's a damn shame."

"But da night didn't turn out to be all dat bad. My knight's name turned out to be Ted Smith. He was a banker and as single as they came. I'll never forget his eyes; they were soft blue and just seemed to swallow me whole. Before I met Ted, I'd never really looked a white man in da eye. So, I guess you could say da newness of it all mesmerized me more than anyt'ing."

"Was he interested in you, too?" I grabbed a rag and wiped off the counter to make Mother think I was working.

"Of course he was. Back then I was known as Chocolate Delight. Thick and slick in all da right places."

"I heard that." I slapped her some skins. "So what became of that relationship? Are you married?"

"Unfortunately, no. He courted me for awhile. Took me to restaurants where da prices were high and da amount of food served was low."

I laughed.

"He bought me t'ings I couldn't even pronounce. I was head over heels in love with stars in my eyes and all dat."

"So?"

"So, when I told my family about him, they flipped out. My parents even threatened to disown me if I continued with da relationship."

"What about his family?"

"His family felt da same way but he didn't care as long as we were together. In da end, it was me who decided to break t'ings off. It was da biggest mistake of my life. I eventually married a Black man and as a result I have two beautiful kids. But I never loved him, so after four years of mediocre bliss, we divorced."

"That's too bad. I'm starting to think nobody ever marries their soul mate. Know what I mean?"

"It doesn't have to be dat way, Child. Don't make da same mistakes I did. True love is hard to find."

I cocked my head to the side.

"You know what I'm talking about. I won't come out and say it if dat makes you more comfortable. But deep down, you know. And I t'ink you should follow your heart otherwise you might end up in an unrewarding marriage or alone wishing and wondering, 'what if'. "

I pretended to wipe down the espresso machine.

"Just a little brain food for your soul. I should be on my way, now. Thanks a lot for da drink." She handed me a five.

I pushed her hand away. "It's on the house. After all, you made it." I smiled.

"Take care, Kendall. And remember what I said." With that, she left me to my own thoughts.

Was Ifa right? Would I someday lead a life of false hopes? Would I ever get that house with the black picket fence and a dog named Pancho? Would I ever walk through my own door with genuine delight saying something like, 'Honey, I'm home?' And would my true love be there to greet me? Or would I be greeted solely by my dog and maybe a cat named, White Cherry? Would I find comfort in a tub of Rocky Road and a flat glass of white zinfandel while laying in a king-sized bed all alone watching reruns of *Martin* and *Living Single?*

"Quarter for your thoughts?" Mother joined me at the counter.

"I must've zoned out. Sorry. You need help with something?"

"No, I just came to check up on you. It's about closing time. I appreciate your help, today."

"Well, I don't come cheap." I forced out a laugh.

"That's pathetic, Kendy. Are you gonna tell me what's wrong or keep it all inside until you explode?"

"Keep what, inside? I'm fine. Just tired is all."

"That's what I been meaning to talk to you about. Now I don't want you to take offense to what I'm about to ask you."

I sighed. I knew what she was going to ask long before the words left her lips.

"Have you been taking sleeping pills?"

"Occasionally? Why? You do it, too."

"I know I do. That's what concerns me about you. I do it to escape when things get stressful. But it's better to face your problems as they come otherwise you'll wake up the next day giving birth to ten new ones."

"I've just been having a hard time in school." I belched out the same lie I'd told many times before.

"Anything I can help with?"

"No, I think I got it under control now."

"You sure?"

"I'm sure." I took off my apron. I mean, even if I wanted to talk to Mother, I couldn't at that point. Know what I mean? I walked out the door and left the pain to drown in my tears.

chapter nineteen

Knee Deep

The Friday following the 'Connie scare', I sliced my finger open on a broken slide at work. Mother took me to the emergency room and I was released several hours later with eight stitches and a prescription for Vicodin. The pain relief that the Vicodin provided was also accompanied by a calm sense of I-don't-give-a-damn. I spent the entire weekend at home either sound asleep or sitting up in bed looking inside myself. I was a mess.

When Monday rolled around, the throbbing pain in my bandaged index finger had completely ceased. But the subconscious pain in my head was still stronger than ever so I took one tablet of Vicodin and headed off to school. During chemistry, the calming effects surfaced then died sometime around lunch. I popped two more pills in my mouth and headed towards the Mexican food line. Hell, I'd be home in an hour, anyway.

"Hi, Kendall." Connie walked up behind me.

My heart started to pound. I hadn't talked to Connie since "The Phantom of The Opera." What the hell was I going to say to her? In my state of panic, the Vicodin bottle came flying out of my hands.

She bent down to retrieve the bottle then handed it back to me.

"Thanks." I placed the bottle safely in my purse hoping that the pills would calm my nerves sooner than later. "Hey, Connie. What's been going on?" My voice shook like an airplane in a thunderstorm.

"Not much. I just got out of English." She lightly fingered the teal bandage on my finger. "What happened?"

"Nothing really. Just a little accident at the lab."

"Does it hurt?" Her finger lingered on the bandage.

"Not really." I snatched my hand away. "I-I should get going."

"Wait, Kendall. Please don't do this."

"Do what?"

"Don't treat me like an acquaintance. We're supposed to be friends, remember?"

"I'm sorry." I sighed. I mean, I couldn't run forever. "I guess I just need to eat something. I lost another five pounds, you know?"

"That's not good. Why don't I buy you lunch?"

"Here? In the cafeteria?"

"We *could* go out but my car is having a disc changer installed. I caught the bus to school."

"Caught the bus? You should've called me. I would've given you a ride."

"I did try to call you. All week, in fact. You never answered."

"Oh." I looked down at the ground. "Sorry."

"Let's just eat here." She smiled.

A few minutes later, we were munching on turkey wraps and diet cola.

"So, what's going on, Kendall? Talk to me."

"Not much is going on with me. Except for this finger mishap." I used a plastic knife to cut my wrap in half. Mayonnaise oozed onto my plate.

"No, Kendall. I meant with us."

"Us? You're saying that like we're a couple or something." I chuckled nervously.

"There are different types of couples, Kendall. We're still friends, right?"

"You know what I meant." I sat back in my chair.

"Let's just please stop this." She folded her arms across her chest. "I'm sorry for what I did."

"I know."

"Then why am I being punished? And was it so bad what I did?"

I looked down at my shoes.

"Well, was it?"

"Connie, I'm still trying to figure out what happened. My head is so messed up, right now. I can't even think straight." My words were starting to run together.

"Well, can we figure it out together? As friends? Because I'm just as screwed up as you are." Her eyes filled with tears.

The sight of her tears killed me inside. The knowledge that I was responsible for her pain made me ashamed.

"I'm sorry for the way I acted," I finally spoke. "I overreacted. I haven't been myself, lately. I'm knee deep in crap and I'm constantly sinking." I joined her eyes.

"Do you want to talk about it?"

"I wouldn't even know where to begin."

"Start at the beginning. I have all day." She sipped on her soda.

"Actually, there's something I wanna tell you. Something I haven't even told my own mother."

"You can tell me anything." She sat forward in her seat.

"Well, for the past year, I've been seeing a therapist."

"That's great. Is it helping?"

"I don't know. But that's not what I really wanted to tell you." She held my eyes.

"You already know about the sleeping pill thing?" She nodded her head.

"Well, it's not only an over-the-counter habit, now." She sighed. "Yeah, I saw the Vicodin."

"You think I'm nuts?"

"Nuts? For acknowledging that you're a human being born into a psychotic world of hate?"

I laughed; it felt good.

"What are you gonna do?"

"About what?"

"Come on, Kendall."

"I'm trying to quit. It's scary, though. I'm so used to the feeling, now." I was already starting to feel the effects of the previous dose.

She reached across the table and touched my cheek.

Her touch felt like silk.

"You'll get through it, Kendall."

For the first time in months, I knew I would.

"Now that we're being open, there's something I need to talk to *you* about."

"Okay." I nervously sucked on a cola-drenched ice cube.

"Something I've been avoiding since the first time I met you. Something that might explain what happened that night. Something that-"

"Dammit, Connie. Don't tap-dance. Just tell me."

"Kendall, I'm-"

It wasn't me who interrupted her the second time. Before Connie even had a chance to finish her sentence, a woman with a heavy voice appeared in front of our table.

"So, this is where you been hidin'."

I looked at Connie and shrugged my shoulders.

Connie blushed and stood up, quickly. "Shauna, don't do this. Not here. Not now."

"Don't do what? You the one who ain't returned none of my calls." Shauna gestured towards me. "And now I see why."

I looked behind me, wondering if somebody else was standing there. I mean, how could she be referring to me? I had never seen the woman before. And believe me, if I'd have seen her, I'd have remembered. Shauna was a dark-skinned sistah. Chocolate brown, like Mother. She was about my height but stockier, dressed in baggy denim overalls, a wife beater and brown, unlaced work boots. Her hair was dyed blond and styled in a short, curly afro.

"Don't do this," Connie nearly pleaded.

"Do what, Con'? I ain't talked to you in four months and you tellin' me not to do this?"

I stood up. I didn't want to be part of nobody's mess. Know what I mean?

"No, you ain't gotta go nowhere. I'm only gonna be a minute," Shauna said to me.

I sat back down. I mean, she was a big sistah.

Connie turned to me and mouthed, "I'm sorry."

I smiled to let her know it was okay.

"Shauna, let's go outside, if you want to talk. This isn't the time or the place."

"How could you treat me like this, Con'? Like a stranger? Like a bum off the streets. You don't call me back. You ignore me when you see me around the 'hood'."

"Shauna, this is bullshit. I don't even go around your neighborhood anymore. I'm working two jobs and going to school. When the hell am I supposed to call you?"

Things were getting too heated for me. I looked around for an escape route.

"You found the time to call me before, *Ms.* High and Mighty."

"Don't start with the names, again. That's what started all this in the first place."

"Don't tell me what started this. I was there."

"You *were* there. Then you left me to pay for the apartment by myself. How low was that?"

I wrinkled my brow. Connie never told me she had a roommate before.

"I left you? You threw me out. And after I gave you five years of my life, too. Five years and you move on, just like that." She gestured towards me, again.

Was I in the *Twilight Zone*?

"Just go, Shauna. Leave me, alone." Connie's face was beat red, at that point. "Can't you get it through your head? I'm not interested, anymore. It's over."

I sat forward in my seat unsure if what I was witnessing was real. That's when it happened; an event that would change my life forever. An event as shocking as the Rodney King beating and the O.J Simpson verdict, combined.

"I still love you, Con'."

Friends say I love you, everyday. But the true shocker came in the moments to follow.

Connie stood with her feet planted on the ground and her eyes resting sadly on Shauna's.

Shauna leaned towards Connie's face. She slid her right hand behind Connie's head and pulled her close.

Connie muttered something along the lines of "Don't" or "Please," as Shauna slowly brought her lips forward.

Then, they kissed.

It wasn't the type of kiss you see in airports between two friends. It was more like the type of kiss you see in movies that involves a passionate embrace and serious lip movement. I was shocked. I had never seen anything like it. I mean, sure I'd witnessed kisses between women as lovers in movies. But to actually see somebody I know, or rather someone I thought I knew, engaged in such a passion-filled kiss with a member of the same sex? I was stunned. Shaken. Scared. And most of all, I was intrigued.

Connie was the first to pull away. Well, actually, she pushed Shauna away and glanced over in my direction with tears in her eyes.

My jaw rested on the table.

"How could you? After one year? You think you can just come back into my life? It's not fair, Shauna. And in front of Kendall. She didn't know, Shauna." Connie burst into heavy sobs and ran out of the cafeteria.

"Shit." Shauna hit her right fist into her left palm. She turned towards me. "I'm sorry. I thought you two was together."

I picked my jaw up off the table, grabbed my backpack and walked out the door. There were a few people staring but all I cared about, at that moment, was getting home. It was too much to take in at once. Did people think I was invincible? And how did I not know Connie was gay? I mean, the signs were in my face, all along. The calls out of the blue. The movies, the park, the 'Phantom.' I felt like such a fool. Was I being manipulated? Did Connie have some twisted plan of getting me tangled into a sick threesome? But, there wasn't a manipulative bone in Connie's body. So why didn't she tell me?

I was way too upset by the time I finally reached my bed. I threw off my baggy, carpenter-style jeans and climbed underneath my blanket wearing nothing but a pair of white, cotton draws and a T-shirt. I reached over and took my phone off the hook and pulled out my bottle of Vicodin. I popped two pills into my mouth and laid back on the pillow. I thought about Connie's words about addiction as I waited for sleep to consume me. Then, I thought about the kissing scene and within moments, I was sound asleep.

* * *

"Dr. Wiggim's office."

"Hello, my name is Kendall Reed. I'm a patient of Dr. Wiggim."

"Hello, Ms. Reed. How can I help you?"

"About a week ago, I was seen at the emergency room for a cut."

"I'm sorry to hear that, are you okay?"

"Yes, thank you." I paused for a moment to collect my thoughts. "I was prescribed pain medication by the ER doctor and I was wondering if I could get a refill."

"You'll have to either get it through the original doctor who prescribed the medication or schedule a recheck with Dr. Wiggim. What is the name of the medication?"

"Let me get the bottle. Vi-co-din," I pretended to stumble with the pronunciation.

"Yes, Vicodin. You're right, it's for pain. Are you still in pain?"

"Yes, quite a bit." I lied.

"How many do you have left?"

"About enough for one more dose."

"Okay." I could hear the receptionist typing. "How about tomorrow morning?"

"That works perfectly. But is there any way for Dr. Wiggim to call the pharmacist, tonight? The throbbing is unbearable."

"I'll see what I can do, Kendall. Can I call you back?"

"Sure. You have my home number?"

"555-4567."

"Perfect. Thank you very much."

"Is there anything else I can do for you?"

"That'll do it. Thanks, again. Bye."

"Bye."

I hung up the phone and waited patiently for the receptionist to call back. The night was young and I was out of medication. My head throbbed and my body felt shaky. Twenty pills in three days. What if Dr. Wiggim refused to give me a refill? I thought about pulling out a stitch or two. That would get me more pills for sure. The anticipation was killing me. I was tired of thinking. Tired of dreaming. I just wanted to sleep. The sound of the phone ringing, startled me.

"Hello."

"Ms. Reed?"

"This is she."

"Your prescription will be ready in fifteen minutes at the pharmacy."

"Thank you." I sighed in relief.

"We'll see you tomorrow at eight?"

"Can we make that later on in the week? I have an appointment, in the morning."

"Sure. What day?"

"Can I call you?"

"Sure. Call soon, though. You know how full Dr. Wiggim gets?"

"No problem. Thanks again for your help. Bye."

Within an hour, I had a new bottle of Vicodin and the promise of a wake less slumber.

chapter twenty

Criminals and Homosexuals

"Why does it bother you so much that she's a lesbian?"

"It doesn't bother me. I told you that. It bothers me that she lied."

"That's understandable. Nobody likes to be lied to. But do you think it was an easy subject for her to bring up?"

"That don't matter. Most truths are hard to confess. Can a murderer be let off the hook just because they made a difficult confession?"

"What do murderers have to do with it? I don't think it's the same, at all."

"In a way, it is."

"A lesbian is equal to a murderer?"

"No. Just the circumstances involved."

"Meaning?"

"Meaning, a murderer is afraid to confess and lose their freedom which is valuable to them."

"Yes."

"And Connie was afraid to lose our friendship which is valuable to her."

"Well said, Kendall." Dr. Porsche leaned forward with a satisfied smile. "Then, why haven't you called her?"

"I don't know. Why hasn't she called me?"

"Reverse it, Kendall. Would you call her if it were the other way around?"

"You mean if I was gay?"

"Yes."

"That wouldn't happen."

"Let's just pretend it did. How would you feel?"

"Scared. And probably mad at myself."

"Mad?"

"Yeah. I'd hate to be attracted to a female."

"Why? Attraction is attraction, isn't it?"

I thought long and hard. "No. That's not true. What about the bad boy/good girl thing? Is it right to be attracted to a criminal?"

"To answer your question, everyone needs love. Even criminals. But is loving a criminal really the same as loving the same sex?"

"Loving? Now you're hitting a whole new subject. I was talking about attraction, not love. And we all know it's wrong to be attracted to the same sex."

"How do *we* know that?"

"By the Bible, I guess. I read it, myself."

Dr. Porsche sat back in her chair staring at me.

"Mother told me it's wrong. Grandma said it's a sin and you'll burn in hell for it. It's just not right." I spoke quickly trying to hide the trembling in my voice. Images of Shauna kissing Connie entered my mind for the hundredth time since the incident occurred, two days ago. Jealousy and anger clouded my mind.

"I'm not going to speak against your family's beliefs. And I'm certainly not going to speak against the Bible. But I can say, by experience, that love and attraction are two emotions we can't control."

I leaned forward, folding both hands across my lap.

"And I don't think God will overlook a genuinely good person because of something they can't control. The God I believe in is a loving and merciful God."

I had the sudden urge to throw out phrases like *What you say?* and *Preach it, Sistah.* Her words comforted my guilt; a guilt that was too deep to explain. "So you don't think Connie is a sinner for being attracted to women?"

"No, Kendall. I don't think anybody can be labeled a sinner based solely on who they love."

I smiled. "But how can I go about feeling comfortable around her, again?"

"Connie?"

"Yeah. After finding out she's a lesbian."

"That's something that'll just have to take time. Start off slow. Call her a few times. Then maybe work up to hanging out, again. It'll work out, you'll see."

"I sure hope so because before all this happened, she was really a great friend."

"Before?"

"Okay. She's still a great friend."

Dr. Porsche smiled. "Always remember she's still the same person you liked before you found out who she *used* to love."

"Dr. Porsche? Do you mind if we cut this session short?" I glanced down at my watch. I only had fifteen minutes left.

"Sure. This is your time. But I do have one thing to talk to you about before you go. Something you mentioned once before."

"What's that?"

"Have you still been taking sleeping pills?"

I felt my ears get hot. "Not really. I mean, yeah, I take a pill or two a day when I can't sleep? But not a lot."

"How often, Kendall?"

I thought about the Vicodin in my purse. Then I thought about the fact that I had taken two pills right before the session. My eyes dropped to the ground.

"Can you sleep without them?"

"Lately no. But that's only 'cause of all the shit that's been going on. I can stop anytime. It just helps me rest so I can be okay for school and work."

"And how do you end up feeling the next day?"

"Okay. At first I felt down and kind of had a headache, in the mornings. But those symptoms went away, after awhile." I looked down at my bandaged finger. "The Vicodin I was given has no side effects."

"Wait a minute, Kendall. That's a very serious drug. People get hospitalized for Vicodin addiction. You never mentioned Vicodin."

"You never asked me what happened to my finger, either."

"Yes, I did. But you've been so spaced out, you probably don't remember." Dr. Porsche was starting to step over her professional boundaries just a bit.

"Tonight, I'll sleep without the damn pills, okay? Is that what you wanna hear?"

"Kendall, you know me, by now. I never want you to say *anything* for my sake. If you want to know, I'm concerned. As your counselor and as someone who's become quite fond of you in the past year. I been noticing a change in you, lately."

"Yeah, thanks for noticing." I softened my tone. "Mother's been concerned. And Daddy, I think. But sometimes he gets so wrapped up in his own shit that he don't notice as much. I feel fine, though. Physically."

Dr. Porsche sat back in her chair without her pen and pad.

"It started last month when Darius and I broke up-" I relayed the entire story starting with Darius slapping me and ending with finding him and Keisha in the park.

"Did you press charges?"

"Nah. I don't feel like going through all the bullshit involved in legal matters. Besides, I just want him out of my life. You know?"

She didn't answer my question. But she did say, "And now you can't stop."

"Can't stop, what?"

"Taking pills. But it was more of a statement than a question. Why do you take them?"

"I told you why. It started with Darius and-"

"No, Kendall. Not what started you. I asked why you're taking them?"

"I don't know. They just make me feel better. Especially the Vicodin. I get so drowsy, I forget about all the crap that's bothering me. It's a nice feeling."

"But what happens when you wake up?"

"Wait a minute. I'm not falling for this mess. The AA lady asked Daddy these questions last year. I'm not addicted."

"Calm down, Kendall. I never said you were addicted. I just want to get to the bottom of things before you *do* become addicted."

"I gotta go. I have an appointment." I stood up and walked towards the door. I mean, how much therapy could one person take? All my problems couldn't be solved in one day. If that was true, Dr. Porsche would be unemployed. Know what I mean?

"Okay, Kendall. See you next week?" Dr. Porsche wore the expression of a wounded puppy.

I hated to be the cause of another's worry but I had enough problems of my own. One person couldn't take on the world. So, with a stick up my ass, I walked out of the office.

chapter twenty-one

Matter Over Mind

I felt like such a fool. It was Friday night. Nearly one week had passed since 'the kiss' and I was standing in the rain with no coat on. Inquiring minds might like to know why, at midnight, wearing nothing but a wife beater and khakis, I was catching my death. To tell you the truth, I didn't even know why. All I know is I was hurting inside and for some reason the acidic drops pounding against my numb flesh gave me a sense of sanity. But let me begin a few hours before I hit rock bottom.

It was eight-o-clock and I was sitting up at The Steak House, one of the most populated restaurants in Dryton, nursing a glass of white zinfandel, that I was never carded for, and pretending to listen to what my lame-ass date had to say. You remember that guy James from the party? Well, after months of ignoring his very existence, I decided to give him a call. I figured that maybe if I dove head first back into the dating scene, I'd somehow forget about Connie. But after listening to James ramble on and on about football, basketball and every other subject I could care less about, I started to miss Connie even more.

"What made you call me?"

"I guess I finally felt ready."

"Ready?"

"Yeah, ready to date, again. You know after Darius?"

"Oh, so you broke up?"

I sat back in my chair, sizing him up. He looked adorable, I guess. I mean, if I was into the tall, muscular and handsome. And he was dressed nice in a red and blue stripped shirt and light, blue jeans. So why was I repulsed by his musky scent and longing for Connie's scent of soft vanilla and cinnamon?

"You mean to tell me you agreed to go out with me even if I was taken?"

His thick lips parted into a grin. "It's not like you were married. I don't think a girl is officially taken until she says, 'I do'."

I laughed. "So you don't believe in committed relationships unless nuptials are announced?"

"Well, I wouldn't say that. I just think if a girl is digging me when she's with somebody else, then she obviously ain't happy with who she's with. Fair game."

"I wasn't digging you, Mr. Conceited. I just liked the way you danced." My second glass of wine was starting to loosen me up. It was Friday night and I was out with one of the most handsome men at Dryton State. I decided to make the most out of it.

"Well, I'm digging you, Mrs. Conceited. Don't you like the way that sounds?"

"What?"

"Mr. and Mrs. Conceited. We're made for each other." He picked at the remnants of his T-bone.

"Is that so?"

"You wouldn't have called me, if it wasn't true. As fine as you are, you could've picked any man to go out with. But you picked me." He winked at me.

"That's nice to hear."

"I'm sure you hear it all the time. I mean, shit, you look better than Halle Berry and Lisa Ray put together."

Lisa Ray? I didn't even blush. I wondered how many times he'd told that lie? I motioned for the waiter to bring me another glass of wine. Intoxication was the only answer to surviving yet another horrific date.

Then, I saw her. At first I blamed the image on wine and confusion. But as she approached me, I knew it was no illusion.

"H-hi, Kendall." Connie had the nerve to approach my table with Shauna by her side.

"Hey, what's up?" I over emphasized my enthusiasm. "You remember James, don't you?" I reached across the table and held his hand.

"Yes. Hi, James." She avoided contact with my eyes. I could tell I had cut her deep.

"Hey," James said.

"And you remember Shauna, don't you?" She cut me back.

Matter Over Mind

"Of course, how could I forget. Hey, Shauna," I said.

"Wassup?" the illiterate Bitch answered.

"I would invite you guys to join us but we're just getting to know each other. You know how *first* dates are?" What did Connie see in her? I was enraged but I didn't want Connie to know she had affected me.

"Kendall, can I talk to you for a minute?"

"Go ahead."

"Outside. I need your advice on something."

"Can't it wait? James and I were just getting ready to-"

"I'll only be a minute." She looked over at James. "Do you mind?"

"As long as you don't turn her against me. You know how you females are?"

Connie rolled her eyes at James.

I smiled at James. A fake smile but a smile nonetheless.

"I'll go get drinks started. Iced tea okay?" Shauna asked.

"Fine, thanks," Connie answered.

Once we were alone, all reservations were tossed aside.

"Why are you doing this, Kendall?"

"Doing what? I'm on a date. A *normal* date. Which is more than I can say for you."

"That was highly uncalled for. I'm not on a date."

"I could care less. You lied to me. I told you everything. I trusted you."

"I tried to tell you. You know I did. I didn't mean for you to find out like that."

"You should've told me from the get-go."

"I know I should've. Please just let me explain."

"I don't see a point. You lied. End of story."

"It's not that easy, Kendall. I couldn't just say, 'Hi, I'm Connie and I'm a lesbian'."

I hated hearing her say that word. "What about that woman?"

"Shauna?"

"Who else?" I was acting a jealous fool.

"She wanted to talk."

"Just like she wanted to *talk* the other day?"

"I don't understand the issue here. Are you mad because I didn't tell you? Or because I'm out with Shauna?"

"I hate games."

"It's not a game. It's my life."

"Well, I don't wanna be a part of it."

Her eyes filled with tears.

It killed me inside.

"You really mean that?"

"I never say anything I don't mean."

"So, you can honestly stand there and tell me I never meant anything to you? I'm not even worth being your friend?"

"You said it, not me." I left her alone to her tears. Deep inside, I wanted to turn back and say, "I'm sorry." I wanted to run away with her into the night. But something sitting right on the surface of my heart told me not to turn back.

"You okay?" James asked once I returned.

"Let's get out of here."

"Why the hurry?"

"Let's drive away into the night. And whatever happens, happens." I held onto his eyes. "And I do mean, *whatever*."

"Baby, you don't have to tell me twice."

Okay, so I was drunk. My mind was cloudy with intoxication and jealousy: madness and confusion. But that didn't justify my insanity, one bit. It didn't explain why it was ten on a Friday night and I was in a parked Cutlass making out with a guy I knew nothing about. And when I say making out, I mean, tongue-wrestling in the back seat with our shirts off and no one around for miles. Self-destruction is a word that easily comes to mind.

"Are you sure you wanna do this, Kendall?"

Don't talk, fool. The more you say, the less I'll do. What was I doing in the first place? Was I going to throw away my morals and beliefs out of fear of who I really was? But who was I? At that moment in time, I felt as if I were floating outside myself. As if I were looking down at my own shirtless, intoxicated body from a galaxy far away.

"Shall we?"

The sight of the packaged, blue condom jolted me back to a harsh reality. My mind reunited with my body to take control. I didn't know James from Adam. What if I were to get pregnant? I couldn't even make the right decisions for myself half the time, so how could I raise a child? And how could I live with myself after giving something away that I've always held so precious as a result of a few glasses of wine and jealousy? Who was I? Kendall Renee' Reed, a pre-Vet major who hated medicine, a writer who could only type fifteen words-per-minute, a nineteen-year-old woman still living at home, and a woman who was in love with another woman. Yes, that night, while making out with a boy I knew nothing about, I finally realized why I'd never been mentally attracted to the opposite sex; I, Kendall Renee' Reed was a les- I couldn't bring myself to utter the seven-letter word. My body decided to prove my heart wrong.

"Let's do this," I heard my voice say.

He tried to be smooth but instead it all happened in a cluttered mess. My pants couldn't slide around my shoes. His belt wouldn't unlatch. My earring got caught on the seat. I had on my pink, cotton panties with the hole on the side. He had on Scooby Doo boxers. A grown man in cartoon draws. It took him hours, it seemed, to get my bra off. And finally, when we were naked, our bodies weren't the right fit. He was too heavy or maybe I was too light. He was sweaty and I was dry so our bodies kept sticking together. I bumped my head on the door handle. The windows were too foggy for us to breathe comfortably but it was too cold to roll down the window. Then, the moment came when it was time for the condom presentation; he ripped it before he could even get it on.

"Dammit." He was out of breath. "I knew I should've brought more."

By the grace of God, the sacred act never took place. It's kind of funny when you think about it. Well, not funny, but certainly amusing. Don't you think?

"Maybe you could-"

"Don't even go there," I said, pulling up my panties.

"Or I could just-"

"Let it go, James. It wasn't meant to be."

On the ride home, it started to rain.

"Kendall, I just wanna say that-"

I silenced him with a kiss. It was a kiss to end an era. A kiss to finally say 'goodbye'.

I closed the door behind me and watched him drive away. Large drops of rain fell from the sky as if to wash away my past. It was time to face the future. Time to embrace my true self.

You can call me a fool. Hell, I'll even call myself a fool. But that night, with large acidic drops beating against my skull, I knew who I was. And most importantly, I knew the answer to a question that many people spend their entire lives trying to unveil; I finally knew why.

chapter twenty-two

Beer and Sour Chews

I woke up on Saturday morning feeling as if I were still dreaming. It was a beautiful morning. At least that's what the average, I-love-the-sun, person would say. But, after a night of reliving the James/Connie/Shauna incident over and over, the sound of the birds chirping pierced through my eardrums like a sharp knife. I grabbed my journal and a pencil, just in case I needed to erase, and started to write:

Dear Reader,
~~I can tell he's been drinking, again. I can smell his nauseating, alcohol-tinged breath whenever he says my name. Like an unintentional violation. A silent rape. And it kills me. Deep down, I can feel my soul rapidly melting like snowflakes on a hot grill. And it hurts.~~

I crossed out my words the moment they hit the page. I closed my leather-bound journal and tucked it safely into my desk drawer. It was time to face the man I spent my entire life ignoring.

"Good morning, Daddy." I joined him in the living room. He was watching the news and reading the newspaper, as usual.

"Morning, Kendy. You up early for a Saturday."

I stretched and yawned. "I felt like sleeping in but the sun disturbed me, so here I am."

"I heard that." He put down the newspaper. "Since you're up so early. You wanna go catch some fish?"

"I'll have to pass." I smiled at the thought. I mean, it had been over ten years since I baited a hook. But the idea of mosquitoes and mud didn't appeal to me at that moment.

"What? You too grown to go fishin' with your Daddy?"

I smiled. "No, I just don't feel like it, this morning. You can never be too grown for fishing."

"That's my girl." Daddy paused. "Well, I gotta take advantage of this moment, somehow. It's not everyday that we're both off work on the same day. How 'bout breakfast?"

"You cooking?" I asked.

He laughed a deep throaty laugh. "I was thinking more along the lines of that House of Waffles restaurant."

"That works for me." I mean, if I couldn't enjoy the delights of Thomas Reed's good ass breakfast, the next best thing was House of Waffles; they specialize in waffles and pancake recipes from all over the world. They have the kind of breakfast that makes you want to slap your mama, your grandma and all their friends. "Mother up?"

"Nah. She still in the bed." He held a finger to his full lips. "Let's not wake her. She's had a long week."

He wasn't bullshitting either. I swear Mother belongs to more groups than the president of the United States; gotta love that Bush, huh? Between her book clubs on Monday nights, Bible group on Tuesday nights and the Association for Young Readers of America meetings on Friday nights, I didn't know when she ever rested. I wonder what the world would be like if everybody were that ambitious. There for damn sure wouldn't be as many people sitting on street corners, begging for shit that half of us can't give.

"Let me get dressed real quick." I headed towards my room. "Won't be more than five minutes."

"Take ten and do something about that hair."

I couldn't help but laugh. My hair was standing up in every direction but the right one.

* * *

Within an hour, we were sitting up in House of Waffles with twenty other people, waiting to be seated.

"This is crazy. We been waitin' twenty minutes, already. How long did they say it was gonna be?" Daddy leaned back on the wooden bench impatiently.

"He said ten minutes, I think. I forgot how packed it gets on Saturdays."

"Who you tellin'? We could've been sittin' up on the couch nice and full right now if I would've cooked."

"*If* is definitely the key word. But you didn't, Lazy, so here we are." I laughed. The room was full of unhappy faces drowned by impatience and hunger.

Daddy shook his head as the woman sitting next to him did what she could to keep her children/animals in line.

"Bobby, don't hit your sister. Christine, don't curse at your brother." The woman spoke in a meek voice with a German accent. Or maybe it was Russian. Whatever it was, it wasn't the voice her kids were listening to.

Thomas. Party of two. Thomas. Party of two.

"Finally," Daddy said under his breath, as we were lead to a booth only a few feet away from the kitchen. The table wasn't the best but after a thirty-minute wait, neither of us were about to risk waiting a minute longer.

"Wonder how long it's gonna take us to get some coffee? An hour?" Daddy said.

"I know. By the time we get our pancakes, it's gonna be time for lunch." I laughed.

Daddy already had the newspaper covering half his face so he barely let out a chuckle. You know the kind of courtesy laugh a person does to let you know *I heard your joke but I'm so irritated I don't give a damn?*

I picked up my menu to make my breakfast selection even though I already had my mouth fixed on a plate of hot, griddlecakes, two fried eggs and turkey sausage.

"Some coffee to start you off?" A leggy, blond-haired woman in her mid-thirties approached our table. She spoke in a dry, uncaring tone and had small spectacles hanging off the tip of her long, pointy nose.

"Ahem," Daddy loudly cleared his throat. "I'd like to order the buttermilk pancakes with scrambled eggs and-"

"I said, can I start you with coffee?" The waitress rudely interrupted.

I rolled my eyes.

Daddy smiled and said, " I *heard* what you said. But I've been waiting almost an hour and would like to get my breakfast started."

The waitress scoffed, dug into her apron pocket and pulled out a writing tablet. "What'll you be having?"

"I want the three-egg breakfast with a side order of buttermilk pancakes. No meat, please. And yes, the coffee would be a great starter." Daddy handed her the menu and dismissed her with his eyes.

"And you?" The waitress turned her body but not her eyes in my direction.

"I'll have the griddle cakes with strawberries on the side, turkey sausage and I'll have my eggs fried, please." I rolled my eyes as I spoke.

"You want your eggs fried?" The waitress asked in a tone above snotty.

"That's what I said."

"Do you mean, over hard?" she rudely asked.

"What's the difference?" I rolled my eyes, again.

"Fried is the old term used. For years we've been calling it over hard."

"Now look-" I waved my finger as I started to speak.

"Lady," Daddy interrupted me. He knew from experience what could happen when a Reed girl started waving her finger. "If we wanted a lecture on proper egg terminology we would've taken the course. Now if you knew what my daughter meant in the first place, why didn't you just walk your behind over to the kitchen and place the order. We've wasted almost ten minutes sitting up here arguing with you. We came here to eat and obviously we're hungry so go do your job." Daddy schooled her but still managed to keep a decent tone to his voice.

The waitress disappeared.

"If I wasn't so hungry, we'd go eat somewhere else."

"Let's go." I threw my napkin onto the table.

"Let's just wait. I'll talk to her manager before we leave."

"Fine. But she ain't gettin' no tip." My ghetto, pissed-off slang started to surface. I searched around the room for the waitress. She was taking the order of an older, white couple sitting a few tables away from us. And guess what?

Beer and Sour Chews

The waitress had a wide smile and pleasant words were streaming from her previously sour lips. By that time, I was hungry and pissed.

Daddy went back to reading the newspaper.

Five minutes later, the waitress, brought Daddy a cup of coffee without so much as a nod to acknowledge his existence.

Ten minutes after that, the older couple received their breakfast.

Within seconds, Daddy was up in the waitress' face. All congeniality had been left at the table with me and his half-empty cup of coffee. "You've been nothing but rude to me and my daughter since the moment you waited on us. And now, you blatantly serve them before us, knowing that we've been waiting far longer than they have. Far longer." He pointed to the older couple who were chowing down on eggs and pancakes, contently.

"Look, sir. I'm doing my best. I can't help it if the cooks are faster with some meals than others."

"Where's your manager?" Daddy spoke sternly.

I stood up and joined Daddy by his side. My eyes were fixated on the waitress with a heated glare.

By that time, practically the entire restaurant was up in our business. Within a matter of seconds, a short, stubby-looking white man wearing a blue, members-only coat and a bad toupee, entered the scene.

"I'm sorry sir. I'm the owner, Greg Rawlins. Is there something I can help you with, today?" Toupee asked.

"You know what? I just wanna get out of here. You can keep the food. I can pay for the coffee, which is all I've had in the hour and a half I've been here. Our waitress has been nothing but rude and inhumane to me and my daughter since we were seated.

"Darlene." The owner turned and glared at the waitress. "Is this true?"

She looked at the ground.

My eyes remained fixated on *Darlene*.

"I bring a lot of business to this joint by hosting my business meetings here, once a week and I don't appreciate being treated this way. Never have I experienced such racism. Not even when I lived in Atlanta."

"I'm so sorry. This will never happen again. I-I can assure you that," Mr. Rawlins groveled. I mean, no business wanted to be slapped with a discrimination lawsuit.

"You're right, this won't happen, again. 'Cause as long as you support people like her, I won't be eating here. And I'll be telling all my friends and business associates about this as well. You can count on that, Mr. Rawlins." Daddy stopped off at the table to grab his coat and newspaper.

We headed out the door.

"McD's?" Daddy asked once we were safe in the roomy confines of his Cadillac.

"McD's? Those nasty-ass egg things?" I frowned, looking down at my watch. "It's ten. I think they're done serving breakfast."

"It ain't over until eleven, I think. But I was just messin' with you." He laughed. "And what makes you think you can cuss now?"

I covered my mouth.

"Yeah, I heard that, Ms. I'm-too-grown-to-go-fishin'-but-I-can-cuss."

We cracked up.

"You think that lady'll get fired?" I asked.

"Nah. And even if she does, there'll be another. That's just how the world is."

"Damn-," I paused, "dang, I wonder when thing'll change."

"Oh, they've changed. Back in Atlanta, when I lived with Pop, it was right in your face. Me and my friends used to beat up white boys all the time for callin' us niggers."

"To your face?" I sucked in my breath. "I don't think I could've held my peace, back then."

"Who could? Why do you think so many of our ancestors are dead? How can a man, truly feel like a man, when he's treated like an animal by someone he knows is physically and probably mentally weaker? That's why Pop is still locked up, today."

Daddy's father was given two life sentences for killing a white man. That's why Daddy had to move to California with his grandpa. But, in Thomas Senior's defense, he killed the white man after he raped his wife, my grandmother. Apparently, while Grandma Yvette was walking home from the grocery store, she was approached by a white man in a pick-up truck. One torn slip later, Grandma Yvette returned home to cook dinner for her kids. She wasn't even planning on telling Grandpa Thomas because she knew what would happen. But, as Grandpa tells it, he knew something happened the moment he saw his wife's face. He says it was almost as if life was no longer present in her eyes. So, one shot gun and one dead, white rapist later, Thomas Senior found himself behind the stone walls of prison. And since Grandma Yvette couldn't afford to support all eight children, Daddy was sent to live with his grandpa, Rick; Daddy was eight-years-old.

"The world ain't changed all that much, though."

"What makes you say that?"

"Well, those white boys from back home used to call us niggers to our faces, right?"

"Yeah? So?"

"So that lady at the restaurant was probably callin' us all kinds of niggers in her head. That's even more dangerous. Even in slavery, it was the mental torture that killed people more than the noose. You know?"

I smiled. Daddy was a deep brothah. I wondered what took me so long to realize it? "Subconsciously, we're killing them, too."

"Who? White people?" Daddy exited the freeway.

"No, bigoted people. All bigoted people, not just whites." I adjusted my seatbelt strap. "In the waitresses head, she might have been thinking, 'nigger'. But you know where she was thinking it from?"

Daddy took his eyes off the road for a moment and looked over at me.

"From behind her minimum-wage-making apron." I laughed. "These two *niggahs* make more in a day than her ass makes in a week. Pardon my French."

Daddy laughed. "Look at my Girl. All grown up into a woman. Hope that Darius is treating you right. I don't wanna have to introduce him to this." He held up his fist.

"Ancient history, Daddy. It's all about my future, now." I thought about Connie. "Let's go home and eat. My stomach is killing me."

"I heard that. But first I need to stop here." Daddy pulled into the liquor store parking lot.

I shook my head. Who in their right mind craved alcohol at ten-in-the-morning? I guess the same person who took Vicodin at eight. It was all about escape.

"Wait for me." I opened the car door. "I want some sour chews."

"This early?" He put his arm around my shoulders. "You got it, Kid."

We laughed all the way into the liquor store.

chapter twenty-three

Hard Hats and Leather

Nearly two weeks had passed since the James incident and still no word from Connie. Since I didn't have a big speech planned, I decided not to call her, either. But I'd be a liar if I said she hadn't somehow crossed my mind at least a few dozen times a day. Once, while I was on my way to the student center, I caught a glimpse of her walking towards me. She was only a few feet away from me and I wanted to run up to her, give her a big hug and let her know everything was going to be alright. I wanted her to return the hug with maybe a kiss on the cheek to let me know she missed me. But, instead I ducked behind a cement pole and speed-walked in the opposite direction. Connie was making me insane.

It was Thursday afternoon, approaching the end of April, and I was on my way to the student parking lot. I was dreading my therapy session because of the way I'd treated Dr. Porsche a few weeks before. I hoped she didn't fire me as a client. Know what I mean?

"Kendall. Kendall." I heard my name being yelled from a far off place somewhere on campus. I knew right away it wasn't Connie because it's not in her personality to act a fool amongst other people.

I stopped in my tracks and turned to see where the noise was coming from. I hate when people call my name out loud.

"Kendall, wait up."

I saw Tomeeka running towards me like a mad woman. I felt like running to my car and driving away but I didn't want to be rude. I mean, I couldn't afford to lose all my friends.

"What's up, Kendall?" Tomeeka was out of breath when she finally reached me.

"Not a whole lotta. Just doing my thing. What you been up to?" I leaned forward and gave her a hug.

"Same old shit, different toilet. You know how it goes."

I reached out and placed my hand softly across her belly. She was definitely showing. "How you feeling?"

"Sick as a dog. But other than that, cool." She paused to tie her shoelaces. She had to sit flat on her behind to reach her feet. "Where you off to?"

"I have an errand to run. Why? What's up?"

"I'll walk you to your car. We haven't really talked since that night in the cafe'. And it seems like we ain't been the same since-" she paused momentarily as if to search for the right words. "Well, you know what happened."

I rolled my eyes. "That's old news. As far as I'm concerned, Keisha and Darius can both kiss my ass. I'm not even trippin' on that, anymore."

"I wasn't talking about Keisha. I haven't talked to her since she moved out."

"Then what're you talking about?"

"'Bout what I said on the phone. 'Bout you and Connie. Remember?"

I nodded my head and sighed. "I thought we were done with that? I don't even feel like gettin' into that, right now. I got too much shit on my plate."

"I'll bet you do. But I just wanted to say, I'm sorry. I never meant it like that. I was just jealous. That's all."

"Jealous? Of what?" I started walking faster towards my car.

"Of all the time you two were spending together. I understand, now. There comes a time in all our lives when we gotta just say fuck everybody."

I stopped walking. "What're you talking about?"

"I ran into Connie a few days ago."

"And?" My hands were on my hips. I didn't have time for Tomeeka's mess.

"And she told me what went down?"

I almost choked. "She told you what?" I mean, why would Connie tell Tomeeka?

"You know what I'm talkin' about. And don't worry, I've

always kinda known Connie was gay. And I don't have no problem with it. I have a gay cousin." She leaned over and whispered, "In high school, I made out with a girl for twenty dollars."

I frowned. How could a person compare someone's life to a stupid childhood bet?

"That girl, Shauna, is a bitch for makin' a scene like that."

"Yeah, she is." I turned and faced her. "But what about all that shit you said on the phone? About me switching sides and all that?"

"Dang. I said I was sorry. And I know you ain't gay. I saw you with Darius. And Connie told me about you and James." She put a hand on my shoulder. "Don't worry. I know you're straight."

"What you mean by that? Why would I be worried? I know who I am." Suddenly my voice felt weak. I began to look outside myself, again. Who was I hiding from?

"Calm down. All I'm sayin' is I've known Connie for a minute, now. She's good people."

I smiled. I had no idea Tomeeka could be so understanding. "I'm still in shock, I guess. I been meaning to call her. You seen her around, today?"

"Yeah, just a few minutes, ago. She told me to give you this." She handed me a card in a purple envelope.

I took the envelope and put it in the bulky pocket of my dark, blue Dockers.

"Well, I better get to class. I have an algebra test that I actually studied for."

"So, you call yourself getting serious now?" I smiled.

"Now I have someone to impress other than myself and my nosy-ass mama." She rubbed her belly.

I laughed. "It was good talking to you, Meeka. I'm sorry we didn't talk sooner."

"No worries, Tramp. You just make sure you do whatever it is you need to do to get better."

"I'll try. Later."

"Later, Kendy." She turned and waddled away.

I sat in my car and pulled the envelope from my pocket. *To Kendall, From Connie Mitchell* was scrawled in cursive on the front. I ripped open the envelope and pulled out the card inside.

The front of the card had a cartoon Dalmatian and said, "Missing you..." And when I opened the card, the Dalmatian's mouth was wide open in a barking motion and it's eyes were drawn as red and white bull's-eyes. It said, "Like crazy." I smiled at the simplicity of the statement. Sometimes the most depth can come from the least amount of words. I started to drive away when I noticed a folded piece of paper at the bottom of the envelope. It was a letter. I unfolded the letter and started to read. It said:

Dearest Kendall,
   I hope by the time you read this letter, you'll have already found it in your heart to forgive me. I'm writing this letter to you in place of the phone call I've been too afraid to attempt. I'm writing this letter in hopes of letting you know how I feel. But you know as well as I do that words alone could never truly express one's feelings towards another.
   I held my breath, almost afraid to read on, but I continued:
   I'm sorry, Kendall. I'm sorry for keeping something from you that is such a big part of me. I wanted to tell you. I tried to tell you. But how can you come out and tell someone you're a lesbian, when you've just come to accept it yourself? It's hard. It's hard when you're experiencing feelings that you've been taught as a child to consider wrong. Or abominable, according to my mother. "No daughter of mine is going to live in sin. It's an abomination, Connie." And that was the last time I've spoken to her. Over four months ago. And a month before that, I told my best friend, well ex best friend now, and you know what she said? Nothing? In fact, I haven't heard from her since. And we've been friends since second grade. Go figure, huh?
   When I met you, I knew this day would come. I knew someday I would have to sit down and reveal my true self to you. You are the closest thing to me since my brother. Kendall, I don't want to lose you like I've seemed to lose everyone else in my life who I've ever loved. And I've lost them to something I can't control. Something I don't want to control.

   I took a deep breath and continued to read:

Kendall, since the first night I met you, I knew there was something about you that set you apart from the rest. I love being around you. I love the way you make me feel when I'm with you. The way you make me laugh and the power you have to make me cry. I love the electricity we have when we're together. I felt it strongly since the night of the musical. And I know you felt it, too. What I'm truly trying to say is:

Kendall, I'm in love with you...

I'm sure by now you've probably thrown this out the window. But I hope as friends, we can work this out. I know things will never be the same between us and I don't think I want them to be. But I do hope you find it in your heart to forgive me for not being honest with you. I never meant to hurt you. All I wanted to do was protect you.

Love Always, Connie Mitchell

P.S. I'm sorry about the other night at the restaurant. I understand why you were upset. Even if it takes you some time to understand.

P.P.S. If you're wondering, it's over between me and Shauna. It was over long before she left.

I refolded the letter and put it in my pocket. Up until that moment, my feelings for Connie, her feelings for me, were locked in a safety box. And now that things were out in the open, I had no idea what to do next. The ball was in my court, in my hands but I had no idea what I was doing. I mean, how could a woman who's been semi-attracted to men all her life, suddenly admit she had feelings for another woman? It was a messed up battle between good and evil. Evil was kicking my ass. I needed to get away. I started up my engine, and drove forward into the day.

* * *

I ended up in Fresno knocking on the door of my best friend's dorm room.

"Kendy? I knew it was you. Who else would bang on my door like they the damn law?"

"I drove three hours to listen to this mess? Come here and give your sister a hug."

Najah was my friend since the fourth grade. As children and teenagers, we were inseparable. Our peers used to call us salt and pepper due to the fact that you couldn't break us apart. And me being light-skinned and she being mocha-colored, the name fit us to a 'T'. As adults, we went our separate ways to college so we never really get a chance to talk, anymore. But when we do see each other, it's almost as if time stood still; that's a sign of true friendship.

"Well, what brings you all the way up here without calling? Not that I'm complaining."

"I thought I'd surprise you. Plus, it's a beautiful day and I just felt like driving."

"I heard that. And with that new convertible you came up on, why not? Ms. Future Veterinarian."

I laughed. If nobody else could, I knew Najah would be the one to cheer me up.

"So, what's up with you? Anything new since we last talked?" She sat down on her twin-sized bed and motioned for me to join her.

I sat down looking around the quaint room. And when I say quaint, I really mean quaint. There, literally, was only one room with no bathroom, no kitchen, no nothing. The only things present in the hot, stuffy room were two twin-sized beds with a dresser in the middle. On top of the dresser was a twelve-inch television and a c.d. player. And I bet she was paying an arm and a leg for that small space, too. You know how universities are. If you don't believe me, go down to the bookstore and buy a single-subject notebook.

"I guess a lot has changed since we talked two months ago. But I'll tell you all about that, later. For now, you can just tell me what's new around here. I like your haircut, by the way. It's hot."

"Thanks. I been wanting to cut if off for awhile now but just didn't have the nerve. My roommate, who you'll meet later, convinced me to swallow my fear and do what I wanna do."

"I'm glad she convinced you, Naj. It looks good." I wasn't bullshitting, either. Back in the day, Najah and I were known for our baggy clothes and long, straight hair. Now, she was sporting a close cut, naturally curly afro.

"Thanks." She patted her fro. "I changed my major."

"Again?" I laughed. "First it was criminal justice. Then psychology. What do you wanna do now?"

"English. I wanna be an English teacher."

"Which age group you wanna teach?"

"High school, most likely."

"But you hate kids. Don't you?"

She laughed. "To be honest with you, Ken. I don't know what the hell I wanna do."

I laughed. At least I wasn't the only one having doubts about my major.

"How're you and Darius doing?"

"Humph." I rolled my eyes. "That's ancient black herstory."

"Get the fuck outta here. I thought you and him would be announcing nuptials by now."

"Never that. Especially not after all he's done to me."

"Wait a minute. I need a little stimulant for all this information."

"You still smoke weed, Girl? I thought you left that behind in high school?"

"Oh yeah, I forgot you were *Ms. Say No To Drugs*." She reached underneath her bed and produced a shortbread cookie tin filled with drug paraphernalia. She pulled out a fat, already rolled joint. "Will it bug you if I smoke this?"

"You know it never bothered me before. Why would it now?"

"Just making sure." She lit up her joint and took a long drag to break the seal. "Now tell me what happened. And start from the beginning."

I relayed the entire story for what seemed like the umpteenth time in my lifetime.

She almost dropped her joint when I got to the part about Darius slapping me. Almost. "He hit you? What the hell. Did you press charges? Did you hit him back? Did Mr. Reed try to pump some lead into his ass? Do you want me to get my brother to fuck him up?"

"Calm down, Naj." I laid back on the bed.

"Don't tell me to calm down. He hit you, Ken." She paused to take a long hit of her weed. She coughed when her lungs reached capacity.

"I know he hit me. That's why I'm not with him, right now. And yes, I hit him back. Damn near broke his jaw with my right cross."

"That's my girl." She slapped me some skins. "Did you press charges?"

I allowed my eyes to focus on a red stain on the beige carpet.

"Are you out of your mind?"

"Come on, Naj. I didn't come all the way down here to relive a moment I've been trying to forget."

"I know but humor me. You know I don't get to talk to you often. I miss you and just wanna make sure you're okay. You been getting enough sleep, lately?"

"Yeah, as much as expected. Why?"

"You look a little tired. Cute, but tired." She offered the joint to me.

I thought about the Vicodin I'd just taken and pushed her hand away, refusing her offer non-verbally.

"Let's go get some coffee or a bagel or something." She smacked her small, bubble lips together. "I got the munchies."

"You always have the munchies. You need to leave that stuff alone. How can you study with that crap?" I stood up and stretched.

"Don't you worry about how I study. I passed all my classes last semester and that's all that counts." She took one last hit before licking her thumb and forefinger and distinguishing her half-smoked joint.

* * *

"You dating anybody, right now?"

"Nope, you know the dating game ain't ever been my scene. I have better things to do with my time than to be worried about some fractious dude trying to rub up on me all the damn time." She dipped a piece of her caramel-drenched cinnamon roll into her hot, white mocha. Her eyes were low from the weed.

"I heard that. I'm giving up on testosterone for awhile." I took a sip of my vanilla latte'.

"Don't give up on testosterone because of one bad apple. I'm making the choice on my own not to date so I can concentrate on school."

"Yeah, you have to keep your priorities straight."

"Don't get me wrong, though. If someone worthwhile comes along I won't let him *or* her go."

I almost choked on my latte'. "Him or her? What's that supposed to mean?"

"Take it how you want." She sat back with a drug-induced grin.

"Are you saying you've turned bisexual?"

"I didn't *turn* into anything, Ken. I'm still the same person I've always been. But in the past year I've opened my eyes a little more."

I sat back in my seat trying to take in what she was saying. Connie flashed through my mind. "Naj?"

"Yeah?"

"Have you ever-," I paused to try to search for the right words, "been with a-"

"Female?"

"Yeah, have you?"

"No, I haven't. Not yet, anyway."

"Not yet?"

"No, I haven't found the right person to." She grinned at me. "To experiment with."

I giggled at the freedom of her statement.

"On a serious note, though. I believe a relationship should be based on love, not gender."

"I never thought about it like that. But you know what our moms taught us about being gay. And you know what the Bible says."

"Yeah, but a human being wrote the Bible. How do we know it wasn't based on King James' own personal condemnations? You know?"

I sat back, not saying a word.

"Only bits and pieces of the Bible are preached about in our church. Just think about how strict holiness churches are. It all depends on how you interpret it all. From what I gather, God is loving. As long as we not hurting ourselves or other people, how can we be sent to hell?"

"Damn, Girl. When'd you get so deep? Those psychology classes really made you conscious."

"Yeah, I guess you can say it's the psych classes. But I also been going to a women's group with my roommate, Nicole. She's one of the first 'out' lesbians I met here in Fresno."

"What's the name of the group?"

"It's called, Zami: Women working together as friends and lovers."

"Audre Lorde? She's one of my favorite writers." I drank the last of my latte'.

"You outta come down and check out one of our meetings. It's not just a lesbian group. It's a bunch of conscious women who get together twice a month to discuss diversity." Najah was still high.

"I might just do that."

"You should. It's good to expose yourself to different ways of thinking."

"I hear you. But what made you go in the first place? I know your roommate didn't just drag your ass there."

"No, I made the decision on my own."

"For no reason, at all? Come on, Naj. I know you better than that."

"I had my reasons." Her lips parted to a full grin. "Growing up, I found myself attracted to both my male and female friends."

"No shit?"

"Nope. I even had my eye on you for awhile."

"Yeah? Why didn't you tell me, then?"

"And ruin our friendship. Besides, you're like my sister." She laughed. "I ain't down with incest."

"I still would've wanted to know. How do you know I-"

"What? *Ms*. Homophobia."

"How do you know I didn't feel the same?" I squirmed in my chair.

"Did you? Do you?" She sat forward in her seat.

I blushed. It felt good to be open. Like a baby bird discovering flight.

"Nah. Don't answer that." She sat back. "Why would it matter now? We're best friends."

"Right." I exhaled loudly.

"Speaking of friends." She leaned forward, again. "Is there anything you wanna tell me?"

"What you mean?"

"I mean, you didn't call and now you're just here. What's up, Kendall?"

"Nothing's up. Can't I just come see you?"

"Course you can but I know you. Something's up, so spill it."

"Well." I smoothed down my white, polo. "There's this friend."

"Wait, I hope this ain't one of those stories where the friend turns out to be you."

"No, Najah. Just listen." I yawned. Damn that Vicodin. "There's this friend I have. We met at a party a few months ago and have been hanging ever since."

"No wonder you don't call me."

"Let me finish. Me and this friend been spending a lot of time together. But it's not like when me and you are together."

"What you mean?"

"Well, when me and you're together, I feel good. Relaxed and like I can be myself."

"Yeah?"

"With me and my other friend, it feels good in a different way. I feel like I can be myself but at the same time I don't wanna be myself. Instead, I wanna be better. You know?"

"Yeah, I understand, exactly. But why don't you just be honest with me and with yourself."

"Meaning?"

"Meaning, say what it is you know deep down you wanna say. I mean, it's obvious that this mysterious person is more than just a friend to you. And it's also obvious that this person is female. So just admit the fact that-"

"Her name is Connie," I blurted out. "I'm so messed up, Naj. I can't even think straight. I don't know what I'm doing right now. Can't tell up from down. And the longer I sit around being self absorbed, I'm afraid I'm gonna screw things up and ruin what we have."

"She know how you feel?"

"I don't think so. I've shown her, I think. But I haven't told her. Even after she told me how she felt about me." I pulled the letter out of my pocket. "Here."

It took Najah longer than the average college student to get through the letter. Say no to drugs. She refolded the letter and handed it back to me. "What you gonna do, now?"

"Crawl behind a bush and die like a sick animal. I did something kind of messed up a few weeks ago. I don't really wanna get into the details but let's just say a guy was involved."

"Trying to prove to yourself you're straight, huh?"

"Something like that. But it didn't happen. Thank God." I stared at my hands. "I'm hopeless."

"Don't get all suicidal on me and shit. What you gonna do?"

I shrugged my shoulders.

"You do know. You just too scared to do anything about it. That's not like the Ken I know. The Ken I know is fearless. Invincible."

I managed a weak smile. "Then why do I feel like such a coward?"

"'Cause you finally in a situation where you don't have control. You're spinning and don't know where or when you gonna stop." She leaned back in her seat with a satisfied grin on her face. "Kendall's in love."

I sat erect. Being attracted to Connie was one thing. Being in love was unheard of in my world.

"Just go with it," Naj said. "It might be what your uptight ass needs."

I laughed. "Hey, Naj?" I stood up to throw my empty cup away.

"Yeah?"

"I really miss you back home. You've always been my second sister."

"Then why don't you call your sister more often?"

"I will." I sat back down. "With your weed-smoking ass."

She flipped me off.

Just as we were about to walk out the cafe, a tall, blond-hair, blue-eyed chick plopped down in a vacant seat at our table. She wore a pair of tan, cargo pants with a black tank top and an exhausted grin on her face.

"What's going on, Nicole?" Najah gave her some skins. "Your ears must be burning 'cause I was talking about you up a storm."

"Talking about me? Good things, I hope."

"Of course they were good. I won't bring up the bad shit until Ken gets to know you more." Najah pointed to me. "This is Kendall. Remember the best friend I always talk about?"

"How could I forget?" Nicole said.

"Kendall, this is Nicole."

"Nice to meet you, Nicole."

We shook hands.

"Najah talks about you so much, it seems like I already know you." She pulled her blond ringlets back into a ponytail.

"Where you been, Cole? I thought class was over at five?" Najah asked.

"At the library. I have a paper due, next Thursday and I'm so stressed about it. My Shakespeare instructor is such a drag. He expects us to write five pages in one week. What is he smoking? Crack?"

I chuckled. Nicole was exhausting to listen to.

"Don't worry, Ken," Najah said, "She's not always this neurotic. Only once a week when a paper's due."

"I'm not neurotic. It's just that I have a paper due, next Thursday, an exam in stats, next Friday and I have homework for Spanish due in two days. I'm so behind."

I laughed, harder.

"Okay, okay. I guess I'm a little neurotic. But it's all for a good cause," Nicole said, then joined me in laughter.

I leaned back in my chair, quietly sorting out my thoughts. Visibly, I couldn't tell that Nicole was a lesbian. Just like I couldn't tell that Connie was a lesbian. I've always been taught that lesbians were leather-wearing, short-hair-sporting truck drivers or hard-hat-wearing construction workers. But I was also taught that lesbians were sinners and would someday all burn in hell. There was no way I could see decent people like Najah, Connie and Nicole burning in hell.

"How long are you staying, Kendall?" Nicole asked.

"Just for the evening. I have to get back home soon."

"What? Why the rush? You just got here, Ken. At least you can stay 'till morning. We ain't even ate dinner." Najah smacked her lips together. "I'm hungry, too."

"Don't tell me you smoked weed in the room, again."

Najah grinned at Nicole.

"Kendall, you've gotta talk some sense into this girl. She won't listen to me."

"Nicole," I said, "I've known this fool for years and she still doesn't listen to me. If you can get her to stop smoking weed, I'll-"

"Go out with me?"

"Back off, Nicole. What I tell you 'bout scaring my friends away?" Najah laughed. "And Kendall, quit talking about me like I ain't here. At least I admit I'm addicted to weed."

"Okay, then get help," Nicole said.

"I will." Najah grinned, again. "But maybe tomorrow."

They both laughed.

I thought long and hard. Maybe spending the night in Fresno was just what the doctor ordered. I mean, maybe they could help me solve all my problems.

"Nicole, don't make me have to slap your skinny ass."

I laughed. Or maybe I could just relax and enjoy myself for one night. I fingered the letter in my pocket and let out a much needed breath of expiration.

"So who's buying dinner?" I leaned back in my chair with satisfied tranquility.

chapter twenty-four

Tragic Endings, New Beginnings

The morning after my soul searching, self-cleansing and relaxation, I was finally ready to face the day. By noontime, the sun was shining bright and a cool crisp Spring air brushed passed me. Maybe it was because of the fact that I hadn't taken any pills in the last twelve hours. Or the fact that I finally wasn't afraid to admit how I felt about Connie. Whatever the reason was, I felt refreshed, alive and ready to take on anything and everything that came into my path.

And *everything* stepped right in front of me the instant I walked through familiar doors.

"Kendy, I'm so glad you're home. We gotta go." Mother greeted me wearing old sweats and a T-shirt. Her eyes were wide and her mouth moved a mile a minute.

"What is it, Mother?"

"Come on. We have to get to the hospital."

"The hospital? Who's sick?"

"I'll tell you in the car. We have to get there quick. I'm so glad you're home." She threw on her shoes and coat then pulled me through the door.

I stopped in my tracks. "Is it Grammy? Kiara? Oh no. Where's Daddy?" I was nearly screaming as images of one of my loved ones hooked up to machines, fighting for their life with blood and sweat dripping from their foreheads, flashed through my mind.

"Sorry, Kendy. I just wanna get there." Mother pulled me by the arm towards the car.

"What is it?" I held my breath.

"It's Tomeeka."

"Oh no. Did she go into labor?"

"Yeah." Mother sighed. "She had a girl."

I sighed. "Thank God. But she's like three months early. Is the baby okay?"

"Kendall." Mother took a deep breath. "The baby didn't make it."

"Why didn't you call me? How long was she in labor? Is she okay? I was supposed to be her coach." I started to sob.

Mother squeezed my shoulder. "I don't know all the details. I got a call from Connie, last night at about midnight. They had to do an emergency C-section."

"Connie? Why didn't she call me?"

"I'm sure she did. I called you about ten times. Left a message each time."

I pulled my cell phone from my pocket. Dammit. The battery was dead.

"Let's take my car, Mother. I know a short cut."

Within minutes we were walking into the entrance of the Dryton County Hospital.

"Kendy, you better not ever drive me nowhere like that, again. Got my blood pressure and sugar all worked up."

"Sorry, Mother." I zipped through the hospital, walking so fast I was damn-near jogging.

Mother followed close behind me. "We not much help to that girl dead, Kendy."

I heard Mother talking but I wasn't listening. The only thoughts moving through my head was to find the elevator and get to the fourth floor: ICU. When I found the elevator, guess who was getting off?

Keisha stepped out with a scared look on her face. Normally, I probably would've acted a fool but in lieu of the situation, I decided to swallow my hate. Temporarily, that is.

"How is she?" I looked Keisha dead in the eyes as I spoke.

"She hangin' in there. Just a few cuts and bruises." Her guilty eyes were glued to the ground.

"Cuts and bruises? Was she in an accident? What the hell's going on?"

"Kendall, Marcus beat her up, again. That's how she went in labor. And his ass didn't even have the decency to call 911. A neighbor heard Meeka screaming and called the police." She sucked a mouthful of air into her chubby cheeks. "They lookin' for him, though. I hope they find his ass, too."

I stood there with the door open but couldn't move.

Mother grabbed my arm, lovingly.

Keisha opened her arms and moved towards me for a hug.

Suddenly, my feet found the energy to move and I walked right passed Keisha's open arms and onto the elevator. I was distraught, not insane.

"What was that all about?" Mother asked once the elevator door closed.

"It's nothing. She's just not much of a friend, you know?"

Mother nodded her head without asking anymore questions.

The elevator couldn't move fast enough.

"How is she?" I asked Tomeeka's father, the moment we hit the fourth floor.

"You must be, Kendall." He extended his chubby, light-skinned hand to me.

I shook his hand, gracefully. "How is she, Mr. Banks?" I repeated my question thinking maybe he was hard of hearing.

"Call me, John. It's nice to finally meet you. Meek's been asking about you all morning. She's pulling through just fine."

I let out a much needed sigh of relief.

"Yeah, it's been hard on all of us. Especially her, though." Mr. Bank's expression turned into a distorted medley of anger and down right rage. "That boy better hope the cops find him before I do."

"I heard that. Before *I* do." I snarled right along with Mr. Banks. "This is my mom, Carla."

"How do you do?" John said smiling at Mother as if he were single.

"Nice to meet you, John. I sure am sorry about Tomeeka. I can't even imagine," Mother said.

"You wanna go in? You can both go if you want." John, spoke to us both but his eyes were fixated on Mother.

I frowned. Mr. and Mrs. Banks were happy from what I've heard. But I guess the grass is always greener on the other side.

Or blacker in Mother's case. I chuckled inappropriately on the way up to the nurses desk.

"Tomeeka Banks," I spoke clearly.

"She's down the hall in room 406. But I think the doctor's in there right now. Wait here, I'll go check," a nurse wearing purple scrubs answered sympathetically.

"You nervous?" Mother asked.

"A little. I don't know what to say. She just lost a baby, you know?"

"Yeah, I know how it feels to lose a baby." Mother diverted her eyes to the white, hospital tile as if in deep thought.

Mother had a miscarriage when Kiara was two years old. Maybe it was due to the fact that she was working so hard during the first trimester. Or maybe it was due to the amount of stress going on in her life at that time. I mean, I'm sure being young, pregnant and starting a new career would be treacherous. Whatever the case was, four months into her pregnancy, Carla Reed was in the hospital losing all her natal blood supply. It was a tragedy that, three years later when I was born, turned into a miracle.

"Right this way." The nurse returned and led us down a long corridor.

By the time we reached room 406, my knees were shaking with fear. Tomeeka was asleep with her head slightly raised. There were tubes coming out of almost every crevice on her body. Warm tears streamed down my cold cheeks as I approached her comatose-appearing form. There was a two-inch gash above her left eye that had been closed with at least eight stitches. But other than the gash above her eye, there were no other visible signs of trauma. I mean, I'd seen Marcus do worse. Her once cocoa brown skin had an almost bluish-green tinge with black circles highlighting the outline of her eyes and lips.

"Hi, I'm Evelyn." Tomeeka's mom emerged from a chair that was next to the bed and extended her right hand out to me, then to Mother.

"Hi, I'm Kendall."

"I'm Carla, Kendall's mom. I'm so sorry to see your baby like this. She gettin' any better?"

"She's okay." Tears welled up in Evelyn's eyes. "Just copin' with her loss, at this point."

Mother squeezed Evelyn's hand.

I wiped the tears from my face then walked over to Tomeeka's side. I reached down and held her right hand which was hooked up to both a pulse-oximeter and an IV line. "I'm so sorry I wasn't there, Meeka." I sobbed quietly and bent down to kiss her forehead.

Tomeeka opened her eyes and smiled, weakly. "Hey. What's all this cryin' shit about?" Her voice was raspy.

"How you feeling?"

"You mean besides the fact that my head is killing me and I have tubes coming out of my arms and my vagina."

I laughed. I thought it was amazing how Tomeeka still managed to keep a sense of humor even though her life was in turmoil.

"Don't look so sad, Girl. I ain't dead."

"I know. And I'm grateful for that. Sorry I didn't get you any flowers or anything. I was just trying to get here."

"That's all I wanted. I was worried about you. Where was you?" She attempted to lift her head but was too weak to succeed.

"I was around." I pushed the button on the bed to raise her head. "Had some soul searching to do. I'm better now."

"Well, next time you do some shit like that, let a sistah know. I didn't know what to think."

"Tomeeka, calm down. You know what the doctor said about overexertion," Evelyn said.

"You heard about my baby girl?" Tomeeka whispered.

"Yeah." I bent down.

Tomeeka let the tears flow. Evelyn came over and joined in. Next thing I knew, we were all hugging and crying.

Tomeeka pushed the automatic Morphine button.

At that moment, I wanted to take her in my arms, hold her tight and let her know everything was going to be alright. But deep down, I knew nothing was alright.

"Get some rest, okay? I'll be here when you wake up." I bent down and kissed her cheek.

She smiled weakly then drifted off to sleep.

I walked outside the room and took a deep breath. The stench of hospital cleaners and death filled my nostrils. The sound of artificial heartbeats and respirators echoed in my ear canals. I hoped that somewhere Marcus' trifling ass was laid up feeling as much pain as he had caused Tomeeka. Actually, I wished that he could feel even more pain than she was but then I'd be wishing for his death.

"H-hi, Kendall."

I looked up and saw Connie standing in front of me. Her light brown hair accented her even lighter brown skin creating an almost transparent glow. She looked like an angel.

"How're you holding up?" She didn't give me any eye contact.

"Good. I mean, okay." I cleared my throat. "I mean, I guess."

"Glad to hear it." She stared at her sandals. "Listen, Kendall-"

I was tired of playing games. I missed her like crazy. What the hell was wrong with that? I reached forward and grabbed her in a tight embrace.

She hugged me back softly at first, then with more intensity.

"I missed you so much, Connie."

"You can't imagine how much I missed you," she whispered, softly.

I was the first to break from her embrace. Suddenly, I felt embarrassed and awkward. As if everything I said from that point on was being recorded and I only had one chance to get it right. Then our eyes met and all I could do was smile.

And blush.

We walked into the private 'grievance' room and sat down side-by-side.

"How you been?" I asked once we were alone.

"Okay. Although I've had better weeks."

"I know what you mean." I smiled. "But I think I'm better now."

"Glad to hear it. I read your poem in the Black Hole. It was beautiful." She sat forward with her eyes fixated on her lap. I could tell she was uncomfortable.

"I'm surprised it was picked. Took me no more than twenty minutes to write."

"You're amazing. But I'm sure you already know that." She smiled, uneasily.

"Means more coming from you." I grabbed her right hand. "About the letter-"

"Look, Kendall, I'm not asking for a response. I just want to be friends, again. I know we can't go back to the way we were before all this happened. And maybe we'll never be able to go back. But I'd like to move forward. If that's okay with you." She turned and faced me.

"Hey." I reached for her left hand, also. "We'll always be friends. And I don't know what's in store for me ahead. But whatever happens, I just want you to know," I leaned forward and whispered in her ear, "I'm in love with you, too."

"I love you so much, Kendall."

"Connie?" I spoke after a few moments of desired silence.

"Yes?" She spoke as if in a trance.

"What about Shauna?"

"Shauna who?" She answered, still in a trance.

I laughed. "Let's go."

"Where?"

"Inside, silly. I mean, aren't you the least bit curious about how Tomeeka's doing?"

"Oh, yeah. Tomeeka." She searched my eyes and found a home inside.

Our eyes held each other.

Then, we kissed.

The moment our lips touched nothing else existed except for Connie and I. Daddy and his alcoholism didn't exist. Keisha and Darius didn't exist. Dr. Porsche didn't exist. Abomination didn't exist. Vicodin didn't exist. At that moment in time, all problems were void somewhere amidst our kiss.

...Soft, chocolate kisses from lips like my own.

We walked down the corridor, together, ready to start our lives in a place where so many lives end.

chapter twenty-five

Sunrays

January 9th, 2002:
"So you're finally finished?"
"Finally. After a year. Do I look any older?"
"Hmm. I guess you can say that. You've matured."
I smiled. "Thank you. So have you."
"Hey. Never tell a sixty-year-old they've matured. That's just another way of calling me old."
I laughed. "You're not old, Doc."
"You're just saying that."
I laughed, again.
"Back to the letter. When did you finish?"
"Last week, sometime. The words came to me suddenly. And it's weird."
"What's weird?"
"Last year when I first started, it was a gripe letter."
"A gripe letter?"
"Yeah, I wasted almost two pages telling him how much I resented him."
"What made you change your mind?"
"I guess the more I started complaining, the more I realized I didn't really have anything against him."
"Oh?"
"Yeah, I mean, true that, he's an alcoholic. But other than that, what's he done to me? I realized he's not drinking to go against me as a person. You know?"
Dr. Porsche nodded her head.
"I'm lucky to have a father in the first place. Some people don't even have that. And he's never resented me for the problems *I* have." I raised both eyebrows. "And you know I have my share of problems."

"Speaking of which, how's the sleeping pill problem?"

"I'm taking it one day at a time. Every once in awhile, I'll slip a pill or two for old times sake."

"And how does it make you feel?"

"Like crap. I have too much to wake up for now." I thought about Connie and couldn't escape a smile. "I just thank God for my friends and family. Without them, I'd never have gotten through it."

She cleared her throat, loudly.

"Okay, okay. Guess you do deserve *some* credit." I laughed. She cracked up.

"Well, I better go. I've gotta get dressed for Tomeeka's birthday dinner."

"That sounds like fun."

"Yeah, after she lost the baby, I've really been trying to be there for her. Especially with Marcus still on the loose."

"I can't believe she didn't press charges." Dr. Porsche shook her head.

"Some people never learn. But she didn't take him back this time." I stood up. "At least that's what she told me."

"Well?"

"Well, what?"

"Are you going to give him the letter or what?"

"I'm gonna just hold on to it." I looked down at my watch. "Right now, I just wanna enjoy Daddy for who he is."

She smiled. "Next month, then?"

"Same time. Same place."

I walked out of Dr. Porsche's office. It had been one hell-of-a year; on September 11th, the Taliban mentally destroyed an entire nation. On April 21st, I, Kendall Renee' Reed, came out to myself.

"All finished?"

"Actually, Connie." I kissed her on the cheek. "I'm just beginning."

We walked out the door hand-in-hand.

Once again, I could feel the warmth of the sun caress my face.

Epilogue

Dear Daddy,

They say the first person a girl falls in love with is her father. As a child, I remember loving everything about you. I loved you for who you were and for the positive image you represented in my life. And I still remember the love.

Remember when you used to sing me to sleep? It wasn't a traditional lullaby that included babies falling out of trees or twinkling stars. And it also didn't include me underneath the covers, tucked in tight while you sat on the edge of the bed bellowing out a melody. You never really sang to me, directly. But every night when you would come home from work with me already tucked safely away in my confines, I'd wait for you to sing. Whether you were singing to the harmonious tunes of Luther Vandross or a beautiful ballad of your own, the sound of your voice always gave me a sense of security. As a young girl, the first thing I fell in love with was your voice. And I sometimes still listen for your voice.

When I was a child, I wanted to marry you, Daddy. And as I entered the arduous world of dating, I chose every teenage boy based on my exaggerated image of you. You taught me never to settle for less. I loved you. But like you've always said, every case of love ensues heartbreak.

You broke my heart, Daddy. Every time you came home and ignored me for a taste of cheap beer. Every time you spoke at me with the scent of alcohol flowing from your words. And I still loved you, regardless of the amount of pain I felt whenever I heard the 'pop' of a can or the 'hiss' of a bottle. I remember as a teenager wondering why you preferred the comfort of a drink over the company of your own daughter. And up until a few days ago, I still had the same question embedded deep in my soul. Why?

Over time, I've realized something: your drinking habit doesn't have anything to do with me, personally. And there is nothing I can do to help you, except offer you the same love I felt for you as a child. Yes, you broke my heart. But in the same respect, I broke yours by hiding the love I've always had for you. I never stopped loving you. You showed me how to laugh as well as cry. You taught me to love as well as hate. It is you who helped me become the woman I am and the woman I want to become. It's been a long journey but it is because of you that I now know what love is; I now know that true love is unconditional.

From the bottom of my heart: Thank you, Daddy.

Always,

Kendall Renee' Reed

Special Preview:
The Drive
A novel,
By Lukwanna Littlejohn
Coming out in 2006

Meet the Millers. The Drive will take you back to the moment in time when afros and bellbottoms made their debut. When, all of America was tuned in to hear Dr. Martin Luther King Jr. give his famous speech, *I Have A Dream*. And when the entire nation came together to protest the war in Vietnam. The Drive will take you back to a time when family was the only way for African Americans to survive in white, American society. Sit back as Papa Miller, a widowed, Black father of four children, subconsciously takes you for a Sunday drive...

Chapter 1

THE DRIVE

I don't remember crying at Mama's funeral. I don't remember the color of the dress I wore or the types of flowers that were placed on her casket in the hot, Valley church. I don't remember what song was playing when the casket was lowered into the ground. And I don't recall the name of the preacher who said the final prayer when the soft earth covered her grave. I do remember the look on my father's face that evening when my brothers and I returned to our seemingly abandoned home; it was a look of fear and worry. It was an expression that seemed foreign to the man I knew as Papa. It was at that moment I finally remember crying. But I wasn't mourning for the past I'd never see again. On January 13, 1961, I cried for the unknown future that threatened the road ahead.

Cancer finally got her.

After the funeral, I spent most of my five-year-old days contemplating ways to hunt Cancer down and ask him/her/it to bring Mama back. I even wrote Cancer a letter, which actually just consisted of my first name, Jordyn, scrawled out at the top of a plain sheet of lined paper and a few scribbles of text that only me and Cancer could decipher. My three older brothers tried to convince me that Mama wasn't coming home, but I still waited weeks for her to return. I remember sitting at the top of the stairs every night expecting her to slip in through the door like a thief in the night. But the door never opened.

Exactly one month after my mama, Eloise Marie Miller, passed away, the Sunday drives began.

"Junior. Tremaine. Antnee. Jordy. Troop up."

"Troop up", was a term that Papa came up with to mark the beginning of our journey. He never had to call my name because every Sunday, I waited faithfully in the mint-green station wagon trying to guess where Papa would take us. Would we go to the lake and eat fried egg and bologna sandwiches with chocolate cookies? Would we go to Sherry's Shakes to eat hamburgers and cola with chocolate syrup? Wherever the day decided to take us, there was always an adventure in store.

"I'm getting too old for this, Rusty. I seen too much to be hushed by a dang-on ice-cream cone."

"You're never too old for ice-cream. And that's Papa to you, *Junior*."

As a sixteen-year-old, Rusty Junior, had already physically out-grown Papa. Standing at six-feet, two inches and weighing almost two-hundred pounds, my oldest brother had grown to be an average, angry black man. He had the same reddish brown skin tone that earned Papa his namesake. And with his hazel brown eyes and sandy brown hair, Junior was the spitting image of Papa. Although, Papa only stood at a little over five and a half feet and weighed no more than a buck fifty-five wet.

"Anthony didn't wash his hands, Papa."

"And what business is that of yours, Tremaine? There ain't no rules for this ride."

"But he was touchin' those slimy things."

At eight-years-old, Tremaine was more of a tattletale than I was.

"Tre', you always puttin' my name in your mouth. Shut-up and quit gettin' in my business, shoot," Anthony said.

"What kind of business could a thirteen-year-old who prefers snails to girls have?" Junior smirked.

"Forget you, Junior. I was workin' on a science project. Just 'cause I ain't no fake-ass pimp like you, don't make me no sissy."

"Yeah." I removed my thumb from my mouth. "He ain't no sissy." I reached over and clutched Anthony's cocoa-brown hand.

"That's enough, boys," Papa roared. "Tre', quit bein' a snitch. Junior, quit provokin' your brother."

Anthony gave Tremaine and Junior the finger.

"Antnee, quit cussin'. You know your Mama wouldn't let you talk like that if she was here. May her soul rest in peace. Especially not in front of Baby Girl."

Baby Girl was a nickname I adopted about a week after Mama passed. Papa and my brothers started using it interchangeably with Jordy; Baby Girl was used when I was viewed as a delicate girl and Jordy was used when I was considered 'one of the boys'.

"Sorry, Pop," Anthony said. He ran his fingers through my light-brown curls then bent down and kissed my high-yellow cheek. "Sorry, Baby Girl."

"Let's just all be quiet for a minute and look at the water. Don't you love the Valley in the spring? Ain't it purty?" I could see Papa's full lips part into a half-smile. Every once in awhile, Papa's southern dialect would shine through. Even though he spent more of his life in California than he did anywhere in the south, his country-boy drawl would occasionally resurface. He was born and raised in the dirtiest parts of New Orleans, Louisiana. Due to racial violence, he quit school at thirteen-years-old and rode to San Francisco on a cargo train that carried tobacco; one month prior to Papa's departure, his father, Jules Miller, was arrested and eventually killed in prison over a moonshine bust.

"When I was a boy-"

"Oh, nooo," the Miller boys chanted.

I sat back, sucked on my thumb and waited in anticipation to hear Papa speak. I loved hearing Papa's stories, despite the fact that they were usually long-winded and exaggerated.

"Hush up, now." Papa gripped the steering wheel with both hands. "Back when I was a boy, I grew up around water."

"I thought it was the swamps?"

"That's right, Baby Girl. New Orleans. Papa Jules used to take me down by the water almost every night. I was about your age, Tre'."

"And he used to smoke tobacco sticks and drink wine before alcohol was made legal. Ya'll went down to the swamp to get away from Gramma." Junior sighed. "Told you I'm too old for this, ya dig?"

"But did I ever tell you about the time your Granpy Jules lost a finger to Willy?"

I took my thumb out of my mouth. "Willy? Who that?"

"No, Baby Girl, not 'who that' but more like 'what that.' You see, Willy was a 'gator. The baddest 'gator in all of Louisiana. And just like the rest of the South in the thirties, Willy didn't take too kindly to colored people."

"Animals don't see no color. Meat is meat. An alligator would eat a white man just as quick."

"Junior, I know what I remember. Willy didn't like black folks. I know this because white men walked by the same water without a scratch on 'em. But I knew of at least five black men who lost a body part to Willy. In the same water, too."

"Kinda like that dog down the street from the school that only barks at Black kids?"

"Just like that, Tre'." Papa looked back at us and smiled. "Back to Willy. The sky was black that night. Moon and stars was nowhere in sight. Pops was sippin' on shine and ramblin' on and on about what he could'a become had he not been born a Black man in the South. While Pops was talkin', I heard rustlin' somewhere in the trees. Since I hadn't never encountered no 'gator, the thought of Willy never crossed my mind."

I looked out the window at the man-made lake. I pictured Papa as a boy and Grandpy as a young, handsome man. I could almost smell the swampy waters of the Mississippi and feel the cool mud squishing between my toes.

"The night was so black, I could smell Willy before I could see him. I was halfway up the tree before Pops even knew what was going on. He was ramblin' away. Before Papa had a chance to pump his rifle, Willy already had a taste of his left thumb."

"Why didn't Willy kill him? I thought alligators were pretty damn fierce?"

"Antnee said, 'damn'," Tremaine said.

"And now you said it, too." Junior winked at Papa. "Shut-up and let him finish."

"Thank you, Junior. I'll tell ya'll why Willy didn't kill Pops. 'Cause Jules was the meanest Negro in the swamps. He could take on any man no matter how big or tough."

"So what he do?" I asked.

"He hit Willy over the head with his half-full bottle of shine. Willy took a mean blow to the head and got his first taste of shine at the same time."

We were all cracking up at that point.

"From then on he became known as, Willy Shine."

We cracked up harder.

"It was the first and only time Pops was saved by the bottle."

The car grew silent.

"A month later, Pops was arrested with liquor on his breath and piss on his pants."

"Papa," Junior cut in, "not in front of the little ones."

"You're never too young to hear about the evil's of excess."

"What's esmess?" I asked.

"Excess. It means doin' somethin' a lot or too much," Papa spoke softly.

"Like when Mama used to get mad at you for drinking wine at breakfast?"

"Exactly, Jordy." Papa sucked in a mouthful of air.

"I sho' wish that Mama could see you now, Pops." Junior always referred to Papa as "Pops" whenever they spoke man-to-man. "It ain't easy raisin' a houseful of kids with no lady around to keep us in line."

I could see tears in the corner of Papa's eyes.

At that moment I hated cancer even more. I wished I were the meanest girl in the Valley and could beat cancer over the head with a bottle. But for some reason, even with four men looking after me, I knew I had to be strong. I was the woman of the house. Mama used to always say, "a man wouldn't even know how to walk and talk if a woman weren't there to tell him how." Even though Papa seemed to have it under control on the outside, I knew it was up to me to hold it together on the inside.

"Papa?" Tremaine was the first to break the uncomfortable silence.

"Yeah, Little Man?"

"If Grandpa Jules had his thumb bit off by Willy, how come in that jail picture Grandma has, I didn't see no missing finger?"

Junior and Antnee snickered.

"Well." Papa paused to clear his throat. "That night, so Mama Miller wouldn't find out about the shine, your Grandpa had me sew on his thumb. And that's why if you look closely in the picture, you can see that his right thumb is a little crooked."

"I thought you said it was the left thumb?"

Junior and Antnee were cracking up.

"Who wants a frosty?" Papa chimed in over the laughs.

After that, all was forgotten.

Lukwanna Littlejohn was born and raised in the small town of Stockton, CA. She is now living in Sacramento, CA where she is studying Creative Writing with a large family that includes a Chihuahua, three cats, a turtle and a fish. She is working on *Acquired Taste*, the sequel to *Dear Reader*.

Dear Reader is her first novel.

To order additional copies of *Dear Reader* and view upcoming titles by Lukwanna Littlejohn, visit the Black pen Press website at:

> http://www.blackpenpress.com

Or you can order *Dear Reader* on Amazon.com

All additional copies may be autographed by the author, Lukwanna Littlejohn, per your request.